# DARK OBSESSION

"Are you sure that you can't work for me, Miss Shepherd? It would be a great favor."

"No, it wouldn't," she said in a breaking voice. "Have you ever heard of a Jonah? Someone who brings trouble, bad luck, wherever she goes? That's why I can't work for you," she continued, almost angrily. "And why I shouldn't even be talking to you now."

David leaned back and let one arm dangle over the chair and he said without heat, but stubborn as a rock, "Now, on the surface that sounds like a 'crazy obsession.' That's what you expect me to think? I'm afraid I have too much respect for your intelligence. I'd swear, right now, that you have a very good reason to make such a statement and I'd like to know what the reason is."

"If I talk to you much longer," she said quietly, "something may happen."

"To me?" asked David brightly. "Do you really believe that?"

She nodded.

# CHARLOTTE ARMSTRONG

## THE BETTER TO EAT YOU

**ZEBRA BOOKS**
**KENSINGTON PUBLISHING CORP.**

ZEBRA BOOKS

are published by

Kensington Publishing Corp.
475 Park Avenue South
New York, NY 10016

First Zebra Books printing: March, 1992

Printed in the United States of America

# Chapter 1

Professor Wakeley, sliding his tray along in the campus cafeteria, spotted her ahead of him in the line. He took a dish of pudding, keeping her in the corner of his eye. She was the student he called, in his mind, the little blonde owl. Since he had a business proposition to make to her, he watched her take an empty table and he took his tray there.

"Hi, Miss Shepherd. Do you mind?" He didn't wait for her to say but began briskly to move his dishes. She made some polite reply, lost in the clatter, and he realized he had never heard her voice, although he had lectured to her listening face for almost an entire semester.

Miss Sarah Shepherd made an effect almost pathetically young, with that slight body, that crop of pale hair, a complexion of baby-fine delicacy, and then the big glasses on the small nose. But he had known from her sedate clothes, and her demeanor and her isolation, that she was not the run-of-the-mill co-ed. And now from the quality of her final paper, he knew even better, that she was what the rest of the class would call "older." Well-along in her twenties, he guessed.

Now, this close to her, he could detect fine marks along the mouth which was, nevertheless, he was surprised to note, a very beautiful mouth, with thin lips, exquisitely cut.

He made play with the flimsy paper napkin. He settled himself. "I wanted to compliment you on the fine intelligent job you made of the term paper," he said in a benign professorial way.

"Thank you, Mr. Wakeley." She was polite. Her manner assumed that this was the total content and end of what they would say to each other.

David Wakeley was only thirty-four and he had long since developed the iron-clad technique for fending off female students necessary to his occupation. Now he dropped the armor. Maybe she was shy. But she was, beyond a doubt, a smart little thing and he had designs, so now David smiled his moderately famous smile, which broke the mask of vague harassment on his nice rugged rather boyish face. An old friend of the family, a Mrs. McGhee, claimed that his smile could charm birds off the trees, fish from the sea. But it didn't seem to charm Miss Sarah Shepherd. It seemed to alarm her. "Type it yourself?" he beamed.

"Oh yes, sir."

"Take shorthand, do you?"

"Yes, sir."

"Summer is comin' in," said David, pursuing his own plan. "Another week and we'll be scattering. Unless you are going to summer school? Are you?"

"No, sir."

"Ah . . . taking a job maybe?"

"No." She was defending with monosyllables. She wasn't responding at all.

David dumped sugar into his coffee. "Travel?"

6

He beamed foolishly. She was making him sound like an inquisitor. But he continued, just the same.

"No, sir. I don't think so." Her small left hand came trembling up to her bread and butter and he saw with a sensation of shock the wedding ring on it.

But he plunged, just the same. "I'm going to write a book," he announced cheerfully. "A history book."

"I read your book about the Revolution," she said, surprisingly.

"Did you? Good. Well, I've got my notes collected and I'm ready. I'm really popping with this one. But I need a girl. Somebody to do the nasty part. And I want very much to find somebody as intelligent about history as you are. I can pay the prevailing rates and I've plunked myself down here at this table because I want to ask *you* to take the job."

She said with a gasp, "Oh no, I can't!" And her eyes came for the first time to his and they were frightened. David was thoroughly puzzled. How could it be that this small, grave, quiet, intelligent person was frightened? It was a contradiction.

"I'd have bet," said David with light challenge, "that you'd like this work. I'd have bet big money, if I had any, that you'd be interested. And you'd find it fun."

"I . . . I don't say I wouldn't like it." Her eyes were blue-gray and they were tempted to smile. "But I can't," she said, and the mouth was resolute. Her hand *was* trembling.

"Maybe I've presented the idea too abruptly," said David a little less blithely. "But will you do this much? Will you think it over?"

"I couldn't possibly do it, Mr. Wakeley," she

7

said, giving him the courtesy of deep and true regret. "I'm sorry. Thank you for asking me."

"I'm sorry, too. I didn't know that you were married . . . is it . . . Mrs. Shepherd? Perhaps that . . ."

"I'm not married," she said in some kind of repressed anguish.

David leaned back and let one arm dangle over the chair back and he said without heat, but stubborn as a rock, "Then you are going to have to tell me why you can't do it. Is it just that you don't want to?"

Miss Shepherd looked at him again with that sad honesty. "I don't want to," she said quietly.

"I wish you did," said David without taking offense and undaunted. "Is it me you don't like? Or don't you want to mingle with the human race at all?"

He was watching that mouth. He saw little tremors in the muscles around it. The play under the smooth skin was fascinating. It took him a second or two to realize that this little blonde girl was pushed to the very verge of tears, that one more breath could blow her into a fit of weeping. She said, "Will you please excuse me?" in a voice near to breaking.

"That was a mean thing to say," said David contritely. "Please . . . charge it up to my disappointment. When I read your paper I was excited. I thought you were exactly right, the whole way you think, your kind of mind is exactly what I need. Are you sure you can't work for me, Miss Shepherd? It would be a great favor."

"No, it wouldn't," she said in that breaking voice. But she didn't burst into tears. She controlled herself, instead.

8

"That doesn't convince me," he said gently.

Her eyes *were* frightened. Then her face grew cold. "Have you ever heard of a Jonah? Someone who brings trouble, bad luck, wherever she goes?" Because David folded his lips and did not speak she was forced to look at him. "That's why I can't work for you," she continued, almost angrily. "And why I shouldn't even be talking to you now. It isn't that I don't want to mingle with the human race. It's that I *mustn't*."

David's arm still dangled and he let it swing lazily. The little blonde began nervously to pick up her purse and her book. Then he said in his warm interested voice the one thing that could have kept her there. "Now, on the surface that sounds like what is called a 'crazy obsession.'" He saw the girl's lips part. "That's what you expect me to think? I'm afraid I have too much respect for your intelligence. I'd swear, right now, that you have a very good reason to make such a statement and I'd like to know what the reason is."

The tension went out of her body. She seemed to slump. She put both hands on the table. She said, "Thank you very much," in that voice on the edge of weeping. But she snatched back her control once more. "If I talk to you much longer," she said quietly, "something may happen."

"To me?" asked David brightly. "Do you really believe that?"

And she nodded.

"What sort of thing?" asked David with real curiosity. Then he leaned over the table. "Now see here. You may as well tell me all about it, right now, because I warn you, I am a stubborn type and I will not give up trying to persuade you to take this job until I have a complete and convincing reason why not. It looks to me as if you've been having a rough time. Tell me. Don't you want to tell me?"

She closed her eyes. Then she said, "I'd like to tell you. I'd like to know what you think. But . . . maybe if I resign from your class. If . . ." she seemed nervous, "you promise never to speak to me again. Will you promise?"

"No," said David calmly. "I will not."

The girl bit her lovely lower lip. Then she smiled. All term she had been the little blonde owl, with the big glasses turned solemnly, the mouth grave. But now for the first time David saw her smile and she was suddenly as pretty and as merry and as charming a girl as he had ever seen in his life. "You *are* stubborn," she said.

"I really am. So begin at the beginning," said he with a wonderful feeling of pleasure. This poor kid, he was thinking, alone with an idea like that! It shouldn't happen to a human being. She hesitated and then she clasped her hands and began.

"About two and a half years ago," Sarah said in her low sweet voice, "in December, I was working with some Americans in Japan. I am a secretary. I had been there ever since the occupation started." He noticed the good mind forcing organization into her story. "I had a date one night and the man came into my quarters for a last drink. It was quite late, into the morning. I gave him one for the road, and he roared off and he crashed and was killed. There was an inquiry into his accident and I was questioned because I was the last person who saw him alive. It . . . it upset me very much. You see, although he wasn't drunk, not in the least, yet I had given him one for the road. And people kept saying to me, 'You were the last to see him alive.'"

10

"Bad shock," said David sympathetically. "But you were not guilty."

"No. I threw that off," she said straightening up, "I made myself feel not guilty. I threw it off so successfully that I fell in love and got married." She put her left hand to her lips. "That was the summer of 1951. We were married in a little chapel. All our colleagues came. It was a rough sort of wedding, nothing glamorous, and yet it looked like the beginning of everything. So we walked out into the air and he . . . fell down dead at my feet."

"Good Lord!" said David, his hair rising. "You poor kid!"

"So," the girl swallowed, "I really had a breakdown after that. I gave up the job. They clonked me into a hospital for a while and finally they shipped me back to the States." Her hand clenched and released. "I was in pretty bad shape. My parents are gone. There wasn't any place, any person who would have any interest in caring for me but my grandfather, here in Southern California. So, although I hadn't seen him in years, I came to him. He took care of me until I pulled myself together."

"He lives in Los Angeles?"

"No. Near Corona del Mar. My grandfather is Bertrand Fox."

David realized she expected him to recognize the name. But he did not. So he just nodded.

"Early last year," the girl went on in a rather dreary voice, "I got a job in an architect's office. It looked like a wonderful job. The second day I was there, a man took me to lunch. The next morning he got word that his mother had died suddenly in the night and he had to leave, go

11

back East. I . . . left, too."

"A pretty unfortunate coincidence," said David, watching her closely. "On top of the rest. I see what you've been up against."

"I'm afraid I really blew my top," said Sarah. "I guess I had quite a relapse. But Grandfather finally talked me out of it again. And so I got another job. This time it was with a lawyer. I didn't . . . I was afraid to let anyone take me to lunch. But one night the boss and I worked late and he'd missed his dinner, and so had I . . . so we ate dinner together. Too nights afterwards his house burned down. Nobody was h-hurt, but . . . I left. I couldn't . . ."

"Now wait," said David. "This is really piling up. Men, eh? I wonder if that's significant at all."

"I thought of that, too," she said and their eyes met and there was that companionship of mind between them. "So when I went to work again I took care that it was a place full of women. It was a store, a fashion shop. I was secretary to the owner, a woman, and there wasn't a man for miles around. So things went along fairly well for a few weeks. Then one of the girls asked me to move into her apartment and share it, you know? Four days after I moved in she had to be taken to the hospital with a rare and pretty horrible disease. She . . . got well. But I . . . moved. And I quit."

"You didn't get the disease?"

"No, I didn't get it," said Sarah bitterly. "Nothing happens to me."

"It happens to people around you," said David thoughtfully. "Is that the sum?"

"Oh, no," she said. "It isn't. After that—" now her story came tumbling out, glad of release, "I didn't dare take another job. Now you can see why.

12

Grandfather is so sweet. I could have stayed with him for the rest of my . . . well, his life, anyhow. But he is a very old man and he's not very well and he lives . . . While it's a gorgeous place, he has to be pretty much of a recluse and there is just nothing to do there. Especially if I can't make friends. Another girl, my . . . my adopted cousin, runs the house and I'm not really needed. Finally it seemed that the only solution for me was to go to school. So here I am. But I have to be very careful, even so. I live by myself. I don't have a roommate. I shouldn't be talking to you."

"Tell me," said David, feeling very sorry for her, "are you sure this jinx or whatever it is still holds? You should experiment from time to time . . ."

"Oh, it holds," she said sadly. "There was a boy in the drugstore, a nice kid—about seventeen, I suppose he was. I used to go in there a lot and he'd chat over the counter. It was just casual but I suppose I got too friendly. He was about the only person I ever did talk to."

"Something happened?" David felt he was hearing a terrible story.

"After about two weeks, his dog died. The apple of his eye. So you see, male, female, even the young . . . I never went into that drugstore again." Her head shook.

"Any more?" David felt his jaw setting in anger.

"Yes, more. My landlady. She was quite elderly and she saw me alone so much . . . She begged me to come with her to a family thing. It was just three old ladies. All we did was have tea and fruitcake. I . . . I enjoyed it." The voice was ready to break again. "So she asked me again and I did go. We had tea and cheese biscuits and it was gossip about people I never heard of but it was people. . . ."

"What happened?"

"Just out of a clear sky they foreclosed her morgage. For no reason, she was dispossessed. She was just bewildered. But I knew. So now I live in a one-room apartment of my own."

"There must have been a reason for that foreclosure," said David.

"I couldn't find one out." She shook her head. "Now do you see why I can't take your job?"

"I see why you think you can't." David was frowning.

"It isn't unintelligent, is it, to notice a correlation, even if I don't know the cause?" She was watching him anxiously.

"No. You're right. That's too much to be chance."

"I think so, too," she said.

"I'm glad you told me, although it's the strangest thing I've ever heard. Nothing happens to your grandfather?" he asked shrewdly.

"No. I'm safe there."

"I can't help wondering if there is anyone who wants you to be alone and friendless. Or *there*, at your grandfather's."

"No. Nobody really wants me there. Even Grandfather wants me out in the world, for my own sake. He thinks I ought to go back to Japan. He's a little bit superstitious. Lots of stage people are. He says I picked up my ghosts there. I think I will have to go."

"There is nobody who is in any way your enemy?" asked David uneasily.

"I can't imagine who," she said forlornly. "Or why or even *what* it is. It's hard to do any searching for a reason because, of course, I have to do it alone. I just hope . . . I just guess I must wait it

14

out." Her eyes watched him for help.

"Will you work with me this summer?" said David sharply. "Because I very much want you to."

"No," she said, just as sharply.

"Will you go to the movies with me tonight?"

"No. Oh no . . ."

"Will you meet me for . . ."

"No. Please. *Not you*," she said and his eyebrows went up and he grinned.

"Well, now, I kinda fancy myself as just the type to make a good jinx-breaker and besides, as I keep saying . . ."

A man's voice broke in. "Ah there, Sarah."

David looked up. Over them stood a tall man, a big man, and on his heavy shoulders rode a head that was ridiculously too small. He was in his thirties, not very old. There was something about him that seemed watchful.

"Oh, Edgar," said the girl with a sigh. "Professor Wakeley, this is Dr. Perrott. A kind of cousin of mine."

"How do?" said Dr. Perrott, shifting a book to shake hands.

"A student here, Doctor?"

"I come up a couple of times a week, sit in on some lectures, keep an eye on Sarah."

The small blonde had risen, too. "Edgar stays with Grandfather and keeps him well," she said. "Goodbye, Mr. Wakeley."

"I'm trying to persuade Miss Shepherd," David plunged boldly, "to be my secretary this summer. I'm writing a book and I need someone just like her. Do you know any reason why she shouldn't take the job?"

The tall man's face was opposite David's own.

15

Sombre, it was also a closed face. It gave nothing away at all. "I should think that would be up to her," said Dr. Perrott. "Want a lift, Sarah? Don't see your car."

"Thanks, Edgar. Goodbye, Mr. Wakeley." She was nervous and anxious to leave.

"Now just a minute . . ."

"But I told you I couldn't," said Sarah Shepherd. David could see into her eyes, it seemed, a long long way. The message was, We might have been friends. I like you very much indeed. "I'm very pleased you think I'm qualified," she was saying gracefully. "I've enjoyed your course. I liked your book."

"I'll see you in class tomor . . ."

"Goodbye, Mr. Wakeley," There was no doubt she meant it. Deep in the eyes, doors closed. "Goodbye."

"Nice to have met you," said Dr. Perrot and he turned and his big body hid from David's sight the little blonde's flight to the door and away.

David Wakeley sat down. A very hard stubborn look took possession of his normally amiable face.

# *Chapter 2*

Late afternoon, alone, Dr. Perrott drove very
fast. He ran quickly out of the smallish town, east
of the big city, in which the college had its being. It
was not far at all, and not long at his speed, to the
sea.

He passed through an elaborate gateway, past a
guard who might or might not stop and query a
car entering this snobbish colony clustered about
its own cove. Edgar Perrot wound through and
entered upon an ascending private road that was
more snobbish and more exclusive than all the
rest. For there was a small headland, and on the
land side of it the great main artery ran to
the south. But on the sea side there was a shelf cut,
and a house lay curled like a shining lizard, low,
with much glass, on the lip of this shelf. The only
access to the place was through the gates, through
the colony, and up the winding road.

Edgar ran his car into a big garage which was
nestled between the sea and the road's end. He
opened a wrought-iron gate with a key, went up
nine deep steps, and walked briskly on the brick
pavement between flower beds, past a fountain,

and entered the house by a glass door. To his right, the center portion of the house was one huge living room where at this hour, latish on a dull day, the curtains had all been drawn across the sea side. There was an inglenook on the land side. In the nook, on soft cushions, there sat a little gnome of a man and across the Camelot board, on a soft stool, sat a woman.

Edgar Perrott took his place on the opposite bench, the other side of the muttering fire. The woman turned gracefully to pour his cocktail.

"And how is Sarah?" inquired the little old man, cocking his head.

"Sarah's all right." Dr. Perrott sounded gloomy and a trifle sarcastic.

"Your move, Malvina," the old man said.

The woman was big boned and well rounded. She had dark hair drawn tight to a great bun on the back of her neck, a tanned but fresh-looking face and very fine teeth which she knew how to show in a wide smile. She knew how to make her eyes glisten.

"There's a professor, name of Wakeley," said Edgar in his colorless voice. "He's after her to be his secretary, help him write a book this summer."

"Did Sarah consent?" said the old man after a moment.

"Sarah did not consent."

"It wouldn't be desirable," said the old man, softly. There were traces in his voice of British vowels, British rhythms.

"He may persist," said Edgar.

"If he does," the old man sighed, "you will think of something?"

"I suppose so." Edgar's small pale eyes watched the woman.

The old man leaned back. "It's obvious, Malvina, that I've won again," he said petulantly.

"You always do, Grandfather," she purred.

The old man said, "But Sarah is a problem, eh? A problem. Yes, a problem."

Sunday evening David Wakeley went to see his mother's friend, Mrs. Consuelo McGhee.

"Davey!" She held out beringed hands to him. "How nice to see you! I was about to write and complain to your mama."

He gave her a fond smack on the forehead. "I'm here with ulterior motives and don't intend to waste any time on flattery."

"Oh well," she seated herself comfortably, "when a woman gets to be forty, like me, she must take what crumbs fall." She grinned at him. She was sixty-two.

"Blonde this week, hm?" David inspected her critically.

"I was in the mood," said Consuelo airily. "And I think for summer, blonde is so practical."

"Indubitably," said David. He stretched his legs before him. "Just occurred to me that you, in the course of your wanderings among the international fleshpots, lived in England during the whole late lamentable war. Tell me, Consuelo darlin', did you ever hear of a Bertrand Fox?"

"Naturally. Fox and Lupino. What you'd call here a vaudeville team. A pair of beloved clowns, hah!"

"I want to know all about him," said David, sliding down in the chair.

Consuelo settled her portly figure. Her shrewd eyes marked the tension and impatience that he thought he was concealing. "If you promise to let me feed you . . ."

"You may feed me," said David graciously. "As if any schoolteacher ever scorned a free meal . . ."

"With a charming companion . . ." prompted Consuelo.

"With a charming and-so-forth. . . . What about Fox?"

"Before we get into that, how is the family?"

"Letter from Mother. She's fine. Dad's O.K., I guess. Life at Watch Hill, you know, as usual."

"Those dear sane people." Consuelo sighed. "Someday I'm going back to visit."

"They'd love to have you," said David mechanically, "if you could do with only one bathroom. Tell me about this Fox, Consuelo darlin'."

"Have you run afoul of Br'er Fox, Davey?"

"Not yet," he said, too curtly.

Consuelo frowned. "Anything in particular about him?"

"About his family."

"Family! Don't tell me you've met Malvina!"

"Never heard of Malvina. Who is she?"

"All right. Begin at the beginning, as you always say. Let's see. Those two were going great guns in London before the war. Fox and Lupino. Americans, I believe, both of them. Never caught on here. So they became more British than the British. Oh yes, a pair of clowns, as I said. Much beloved by the public, so the public was told. Baggy pants, red nose . . . that's the type. Old-timers, and the second generation was supposed to love them for nostalgic reasons. God knows I saw no others."

David stirred.

"But family, you say. Now, Davey, they weren't

20

what you'd call family men. Let's see. Lupino managed to have a son, and something dreadful happened to him although I can't remember what it was, at this moment. And I believe Fox's solitary daughter had the good sense to run away with an American and fly to this continent. That's really about all I know about family. Of course there's Malvina. Malvina Lupino, she'd be the grand-daughter of Tweedledum. *She's* holding forth down near Corona del Mar, in case you don't realize."

"I realize Bertrand Fox lives down there."

"Oh, you do? That's right, Davey. He's holed up in the darnedest most fabulous house. You see, as I get it from the neighbors, first the blitz came along and did away with Lupino, breaking up the act. So Fox took off, in sorrow, to Ireland for the duration. Taking Malvina along, I believe. I've heard she was a nasty little piece, even then. Now, after the war, lo if it didn't turn out that Fox, years ago, made American investments and guess what the old Fox had done. Bought California land! Of all things! So, he appears and collects, because you know as well as I do what happened to California land values. And now he is living in luxury and ease on the side of a hill. The Nest, he calls his place."

"Do you know, Consuelo darlin', you don't sound as if you liked this Fox much." David looked more pleased than not.

"I never did and I don't now." Consuelo said indignantly. "The old potentate won't let me in."

"What do you mean?"

"He's supposed to be in delicate health. He is to be seen by appointment only. They dole out five minutes of his precious company to deserving folks who bring their pedigrees. Well now, naturally, after having met him before, to the extent of having spent a week end at the same house once, I sprazzed myself up and went to call. Seems Mr. Bertrand Fox was so sorry. He couldn't see me. So there I am, down there for two months every summer and other townspeople get in, but not me. So I'm burned up, Davey, and that's the fact."

"You sure are," said David grinning. "And do I gather that you aren't crazy about Malvina either?"

"Her," snorted Consuelo. "I've seen her about. Buxom lass, Malvina. Comes down from the heights and bows to the commoners. I can't stand her, Davey, any more than her grandfather, and that's the fact, too."

"Grandfather?" said David. "I thought you said . . ."

"Lupino, I meant. Although she is Fox's *adopted* granddaughter, I believe, at that. Relict of his beloved partner. I guess he fished her out of the blitz to be his handmaiden. She acts like the Duchess of Orange. Orange County, that is."

David laughed. "Bitter," he teased.

Consuelo's big handsome face was perfectly cheerful. "The worse thing is, I never did give a darn whether I saw the old man. I wanted to see the house. That house . . ."

"Never mind the house for now. Tell me who Sarah Shepherd is."

"Shepherd. Oh yes. That's his real grand-daughter."

"That's her married name?"

"I dunno, Davey. Shepherd could be the name of the man that Foxey's daughter ran off with, for all

22

I remember. Was it now?" Consuelo's tongue licked her upper plate thoughtfully.

"You've seen her down there?"

"I can't say as I have. Heard of her. I'm on the community grapevine."

"Naturally. Who is Dr. Perrott?"

"I've seen him, all right. He's on view in any of the better bars."

"Much of a practice, has he?"

"None at all. He is just Fox's tame doctor, as far as I know. Big chap with a pinhead?"

"That's the one."

"Are you working around to telling me why all these questions?"

"Soon," said David, cautiously. "But give me more of the background. Clowns, you say?"

"Oh Lord, yes. The beloved clown, which is a folk figure I can't abide. I'll tell you what kind of people they were." Consuelo bounced on the sofa. "I'll give you a for-instance. This house party. Fox and Lupino and assorted members of their families had been asked. Country doctor with a rich wife, friends of mine." Consuelo went off on a sudden tangent. "I may have met Fox's daughter, Davey. If so, she didn't made a very vivid impression. What did is the scene we had. Oh me! It seems that dear Fox and Lupino had promised themselves for some big charity do. I want you to get the picture. There were lots of other acts. The town was crammed with visiting talent. Got that?"

"I've got it."

"Now, in the afternoon before this performance there was an accident. Lupino was struck in the chest by an arrow. A child's arrow. A pure accident. But oh what a lot of blood and commotion! It's the commotion that I remember.

23

The swooning and wailing. 'The show must go on.' For the life of me, I can't see why. Who says so? If it had been a question of a great star around whom many other people had their economic being . . . then I might concede that the show must go on," blustered Consuelo. "But not when it was the kind of thing it actually was. Nothing would have happened . . . nothing, believe me . . . if Lupino had quietly gone to bed on doctor's orders like any other human being. People understand these things. No one would have held it against him. It wasn't worth any commotion. But do you know what that old man . . . he was sixty, if he was a day . . . actually did? Had himself plastered up and went on and did his ridiculous pratt falls and all the rest of it. And everyone carried on as if he were a hero of the greatest proportions. I was disgusted. Nobody gave a second thought to the child. Except me. I remember laying down the law to her father, I think it was, and finally persuading him to take the child out of all the commotion, at least, so she'd not get the idea she'd as good as assassinated the King. Do you get the picture, Davey? Small, narrow little men engrossed with reputation, swollen with self-importance. That Lupino! Although he was no worse than Fox. There wasn't a pennyworth of difference between them."

"And he won't let you in, either," said David, dead pan.

"Exactly," said Consuelo. "Now then, what's all this?"

"I wanted your biased opinion before I told you."

"You got it. For heaven's *sakes* . . ."

He began, rather soberly, with Sarah Shepherd

and the strange sequence of events she had recounted.

"Hm," said Consuelo when he came to a stopping place. "But you know, Davey, granted that guilt-thing she had about the man who crashed, and then the blow when her bridegroom died . . . don't you suppose there could be some distortion in that story?"

"Possibly," he agreed, watching her.

"All of us know people who have had bad luck. We don't relate it to ourselves. Maybe she leaves out certain friends who haven't had bad luck at all. Just as nobody ever tells you when a white cat crosses his path."

"Possibly," admitted David. "I don't know. Don't know *her*. But I told you she wrote such a fine paper . . ."

"Oh come now, Davey. Surely you know intelligence hasn't got a lot to do with emotional stability." He cocked his brow at her. "Well, sometimes not," said Consuelo. "Mad genius, and all that."

David said grimly, "Then you would take it all with a grain of salt?"

"I would. I surely would," said Consuelo comfortably.

"Let me continue. The next day she wasn't in class. Didn't come back at all. Well, that seemed too bad. So I began to hunt around for her. Friday I found her, having lunch with this Dr. Perrott. Nothing daunted, I barged in on them. I can be stubborn . . ."

"Oh yes, you can. Spitting image of your Grandmother James and a more stubborn old . . ."

"Don't get off the track. Listen. She tried to brush me off, of course. But the doctor sat tight and

I didn't brush. Had quite a talk."

"You and Dr. Perrott and the girl, eh?" Consuelo blinked. "What did you talk about, *à trois?*"

"My book," said David promptly.

Consuelo rolled her eyes. "You mean, *you* talked. And your own shop, at that. I bet they got to say goodbye, maybe."

"About all she said was goodbye, again," David admitted. "The doctor said little or nothing. However, she was fascinated by my project. She sparked right up, as I knew she would. When I got to telling her some of the fabulous goings-on in those early days . . ."

"Everything about California is fabulous, as everybody knows. Don't you get off the track. Tell me, is she pretty, Davey?"

"No," said David impatiently. "Yes. Maybe. I don't know. She's just a little blonde girl. I'm not . . . What I wanted more than ever on Friday was to get her to work with me. And it looked as if the only thing standing in the way was this . . ."

"Superstition? Obsession?"

". . . thing," said David. Consuelo looked sharply at him.

"Now it comes out," she pounced.

"Yes. Now, I'll tell you. Last night I parked my car on the hill, as I have to do. I turned the wheels into the curb. I set the brake. I was taking a bath when the car shook loose and rolled down and smashed itself up."

"Oh, Davey! Too bad!"

"I'm afraid that's not the worst of it," David said gently. "I can't make this easy. It killed a woman, Consuelo."

*"Oh!"* She held her powdered cheeks.

"Somebody's maid. Just an innocent woman, going home in the early evening. She must have frozen. She just didn't get out of the way in time. Now, Consuelo, will you consider, with me, the peculiar fact that this accident happens to me right after I try to take up with a girl who thinks she is a Jonah? Now that's odd, surely."

"Odd!" said Consuelo. Now she touched his hand and found it tense. "Davey, you are good and mad, aren't you?"

"I am," said David. "I am good and mad. *I'm* no scared girl with a foolish feeling of guilt on my mind or a shock of sorrow riding *me*. I *know* I set that brake, I cramped those wheels. I won't, for the rest of my life, wonder whether I did or not. I won't carry that burden."

"But if you did?"

"Uh huh," said David. "In the light of the fact that I *did* park my car correctly, now look back on the stuff she told me. What if somebody is fixing these disasters?" Consuelo stared at him. "I'd say," he went on, "that the man crashing, her husband dying . . . all the deaths were . . . well, call them real accidents. But when her lunch date's mother died, too . . . a pure coincidence . . . and Sarah Shepherd went into a tailspin, as who could blame her, suppose *at that point* somebody saw how this notion of hers could be encouraged and . . . well . . . validated? Since then, look. A fire. A disease. Well, there's such a thing as a germ, you know. Then a dog dies. A landlady lost her house. No deaths in that lot. Just disaster. So murder they don't do. They could have done everything else."

"Who could?"

"I don't know."

"Why would they?"

"I don't know. Going to see if I can find out."

Consuelo's girdle creaked and she sighed.

"Because, my sainted courtesy-aunt Consuelo, murder they don't set out to do. But whoever released the brakes on my car last night and swung the wheels so that the car could roll, must have known the risk but didn't mind very much. And *my car* murdered that poor woman. Let me tell you, if it happened because somebody is having fun-and-games with Miss Sarah Shepherd, somebody is going to be sorry."

"Oh dear," said Consuelo. "Oh dear, Davey. Will you be in trouble about the car?"

"I don't think so. And since Prexy pulled all the wires he could, the school isn't mentioned, and my name is misspelled in the papers. So far. But the point is, no one was seen, no evidence was found, and although I am honest and of good repute and they don't doubt my word, the implication remains. *Maybe* I just absent-mindedly, this one time, did not park my car as I thought I had." David had on his rocklike look. "Consuelo, *I know I did.* So . . . well, there's that poor kid . . ."

"But Davey, you know you haven't checked any of her story. Suppose she is in an unhealthy emotional state?"

"Doesn't matter." David looked stubborn. Either way, that girl's in a spot. If she's imagining . . . or if there is some kind of plot going on around her."

"So?" said Consuelo with foreboding.

"She's hasn't got anybody . . ."

"Got her own people."

"Ah . . . has she?" David quoted softly. "'I do not like thee, Dr.' . . . Perrott. Consuelo, be the good scout you always are. Lend me a car. And you're going down there to your beach house soon. Invite me."

"Take the Ford. You're invited."

"That's my darlin'. Meantime, I am going to call on Foxey Grandpa."

"You won't get in," she said, rather alarmed.

"I'll get in," said David. "I want to see those people. I want to know their version of Sarah's story. And if *they* are fixing this jinx to work the way it seems to."

"But Davey, why would they?"

"Don't see why. What I do see is this. Sarah Shepherd doesn't know anyone else. Who else could care? Believe me, Consuelo, if they are behind it and think they can cast me as a minor victim in their little series . . ."

"It's not pretty, what you're thinking."

"It's as vicious an idea as I ever had." David sounded cheerful.

But Consuelo said, "Davey, you are awful mad?"

He nodded.

Consuelo was silent. Finally she roused and said, "There's a lot of money some place, and money, you know, is a gladsome thing. I know a lawyer . . ."

"I knew you'd spark up on this," said David gratefully.

Consuelo said, "I never thought I was a vindictive woman, but he should have let me in."

# Chapter 3

As Consuelo had predicted, the guard at the Colony gates knew her smart red Ford and made no question when David drove through. Around the Colony Cove the houses were heaped, clinging and jutting from the slopes, each beautifully designed and stunningly executed. Life within the Colony and on its private crescent of sand must, he thought, be golden altogether. But he wound to his right, all through this to the other side of the cove, and ascended along a switchback road toward the shelf cut into the hill.

Opposite a three-car garage there was a wide paved apron and he parked there. The shelf itself was above him still, by a few feet, and he could not see the house. An iron fence crossed between the corner of the large garage and the high bluff of the hill. The place was quite a fortress. David thought to himself of knights and dragons and imprisoned maidens and was somewhat amused. He strode to the gate, which was locked, saw the telephone in its box. A female voice answered, "Yes?"

"I'm calling on Miss Shepherd," said he crisply. "David Wakeley."

"A moment, sir." The voice reacted to his assurance with respect.

But it was a long moment. David stood by the gate and he could hear the surf on the rocks at the foot of the headland. He was not high, perhaps no more than fifty feet, but by turning his head over his left shoulder he received a stunning panorama of coast and ocean. Staring back entranced, he heard no one approaching until a woman said softly, "Mr. Wakeley?"

Startled, he looked around. "I am Malvina Lupino. You came to see Sarah? Did she make the appointment?"

"How do?" said David, cheerful and assured. "Surely Miss Shepherd is here?"

"She's on the beach. I'm sorry."

"Then how do I get to the beach?" David smiled at her.

"But you can't get to our beach," the woman said. "I can't really . . . If you would call on the telephone perhaps a little later . . . ?"

This woman, standing the other side of the patterned iron, was tall. David was a tall man but she made him assert his size. He fixed his feet and became immovable and persistent. "I teach at Lowell College," he said rather bluntly as if he felt it high time she realized who he was. "As a matter of fact, I'd like very much to talk to Mr. Fox, or perhaps to you, about Miss Shepherd."

"Professor Wakeley. Of course," Malvina said in her smooth purring voice. She began to do things to the gate. "Grandfather never sees anyone without prearrangement but of course . . . Sarah's teacher . . . If there is anything *I* can do. You must understand," she went on, unlocking the gate, "our reasons for this sort of thing. Grandfather is

32

old and frail and we protect him from even the least surprise, lest we lose him entirely."

"I promise not to shout or throw things," David said, a little shocked. "But I do want to talk to someone who is concerned about Sarah."

"We are all concerned about Sarah," she said softly, letting him in.

They walked together up some steps. David drew a sharp breath. The low house lay on the edge and its barrier, and certain walls, enclosed this garden paved, in part, like a Spanish courtyard, planted with flowers and small graceful trees, dreaming and drowsing between the house and the high bluff upon which blazed and hung curtains and cascades of blossoms. Over the garden's hush the surf still sounded, far away. David felt it in all his muscles, as if he had come into a spot so beautiful and peaceful that it was relaxing to the point of nearly making him fall limply down.

But Malvina led him to some garden chairs in a spot dappled with shade. She was polite, correct, even agreeable, yet by something furtive and stolen in the very tension of her smile, by the glance of her measuring eye toward the house wall, she now made him feel like a criminal intruder. It was as if she had smuggled him within the gate illegally and as if something dreadful would happen were he to be seen or heard.

"You know who Grandfather is, Mr. Wakeley?" Her smile was as pretty as toothpaste and her eyes glistened cordially. But David stiffened. He had seen, before, a frank and open countenance, worn upon a manner that hints of perils and mysteries. He thought she had the candid stare of the pathological liar. He thought he had better be careful.

33

"He is the Fox of Fox and Lupino, isn't he?" David answered easily.

"Yes. He is." Malvina looked down at her large handsome hands. Although her well-fleshed body was not girlish, he thought she was probably only in her twenties. "He is a dear old man, a great darling. They were not so well known in America." Her eyes came up, inquiring.

"Frankly," he admitted, "I never heard of them until I met Sarah."

"Weren't you in England, then, during the war?" she asked. Her arm was graceful.

"I was chair-borne in Washington during the war. I've never been to England." He thought she sighed. "Surely you're not homesick, Miss Lupino?"

She looked around at Paradise. "Sometimes," she said wistfully. David thought to himself, She's suggestible. A strange person. There was something unreal about Malvina, as if she wore a heavy mask and whatever woman existed behind it was not to be easily discovered. "But what is it about Sarah, please?" Malvina purred. "How can I help you?"

David said, "Perhaps you know that she's got a very strange idea that she is a Jonah, a bad luck carrier."

"Oh yes," said Malvina quickly. "Yes, we know." David could not tell whether she *was* alarmed or meant to *seem* a little alarmed. "Such a strange idea," she murmured.

"I want her to work with me on a book this summer. A great boon to me. But this strange idea," David went along with it, "seems to be in the way. I came to see whether her family knew about it."

34

"Oh yes, we do know."

"What do you think of it?"

Malvina hesitated. She threw him a look which seemed to say, Forgive me, but I don't know you. "We know about it," she said firmly, "and we are trying to help her. I doubt if I could persuade her to take that job, Professor Wakeley. I doubt if she should. I think you must get someone else. Surely you can find a secretary who will not trouble you with . . ."

". . . an idea," said David. He settled back, looking his largest and most imperturbable. He was not going to tell Malvina about his car crashing and the tragedy. He was not going to tell Fox, either. He was not ever going to let Sarah Shepherd know about it, if he could help it. "It won't trouble me," he said.

"But aren't you afraid . . ." she began and stopped herself.

"Of an idea?" said David. "No."

He watched her move her hand in a gesture of wonder and helplessness. If the family's version of Sarah's trouble was that it existed only as an idea, he was going to find that out. "Tell me," he said bluntly, "have you thought of psychiatric help?"

"Grandfather is very much opposed to that sort of thing," said Malvina primly as her eyes wandered to a flower. "But I wonder . . ."

David was feeling rather smug and proud of himself for having put her in a position where she would have to tell him the family version, when she suddenly gave him a rather roguish glance. ". . . whether you have a romantic interest in my little cousin?" she said.

It was his turn to look at the flowers. Some instinct told him to be careful. He thought he

35

wouldn't say yes and he wouldn't say no. He glanced at Malvina sidewise. "I am a man who's got a book to write, Miss Lupino. Sarah is my student and I respect her intelligence. I feel sure she would do the work well and enjoy it. And I am not frightened. May I speak to your grandfather?"

Malvina said, a little breathlessly, "I really don't know what to say. I think I must . . ." She rose. David rose.

Somebody clanged the iron gate and Dr. Perrott, coming up the steps, rose into the garden.

"Oh," he said.

"Oh Edgar, there you are. You've met, I see. Will you be nice to Professor Wakeley?" said Malvina prettily. "I am going to see if possibly Grandfather will receive him. He's come about Sarah." The turn of her head, the flutter of her eye all hinted a warning, in spite of her surface grace and bland ease.

Edgar Perrott nodded rather gloomily. He watched her go. He took her chair. "Where is Sarah?" he asked almost suspiciously.

"On the beach, Miss Lupino tells me."

"Been here long?" The doctor's eyes had lightning in them.

"Not long," said David, wondering.


Malvina went through the glass door and into the great center room. She crossed its expanse of quiet carpeting toward the sea side. She knocked lightly on a door at the right and opened it and went through.

This smallish room was a hexagon. It was half glass. The view was astonishing. From this lair, this lookout, this bubble on the cliff's brow, a vast world of water and land lay visible and, through the glare-proof tinted glass, uncannily clear. The old man overlooked it all.

The old man lay in an easy chair. Music was playing. He was sipping and nibbling. His face was craggy and sly and quite contented. "Who came in the red car, Malvina? Eh?" he said, licking his finger.

"David Wakeley." She spoke bluntly. "He wants to talk about Sarah. He's very persistent, Grandfather."

"Dear me," said the old man. "Edgar's device, the accident then, had no effect at all?"

"He makes nothing of that," she said, her breast heaving. "He is not frightened."

"Do you mean he simply came here?"

"I couldn't refuse him at the gate. He would only have got round the rock at low tide and found Sarah on the beach. He wants to know if we have thought of a psychiatrist. Will you see him? What shall I say?" She walked up and down on the rug.

The old man turned his lips in. "Now we knew it would happen one day, Malvina," he soothed. "It merely means that something must be done to solve the problem of Sarah. You and Edgar have been hesitant and squeamish. I have always thought half-measures were weak measures. I am tired of them, Malvina."

"I'm tired, too," she said. "Tired of Edgar's mooning. Tired of watching Sarah all the time. Tired of worrying. I'd like to get away."

"It's been long enough," the old man said, "since the day she came to the gate, looking so ill and wretched that our silly old Mrs. Nepper, that

37

we had then, let her in. Since that moment I walked toward her and thought I was reprieved." The old hands plucked at his clothing.

"What's to be done?" Malvina cried.

"Malvina," cooed the old man, "it was clever of us to get away in all that wartime confusion, to remember about the property, to convince everyone . . . to get all this distance and now have here our inner keep, where no one can come upon me. But we have not been clever about Sarah, you know."

"You've been too clever," she said sulkily.

"I?"

"She'd have gone far away, long ago, Grandfather, if you didn't contradict everything we do. You are too gentle and kind. She thinks you love her."

"Ah," said the old man, "she loves *me*, you mean. Yes, I believe so."

"I think we've been lucky," she said gloomily, "so far."

"Lucky?" The old man did not respect the idea of luck. "Perhaps. Certainly on the day she came, that I was wearing a coat and a waistcoat. She did not distinguish Fox from Lupino after all these years. Few alive will ever come our way who could." The old man pulled at his shirt. "But Sarah . . . Sarah, if anyone in this world . . . would have known the scar on Lupino's breast . . ." his chin went down on his breastbone, "since she made it herself, that wicked child, with her bow and arrow."

"Something must be done, Grandfather," said Malvina, impatient with the past. "Can't you be cross with her?"

"Weak measures," the old man said. "Frighten

38

her. Send her away. 'Perhaps' we have said to ourselves. 'Perhaps' she does not remember the incident at all. But 'perhaps' is a weak word, Malvina. And so we couldn't risk a chum, a gossip, a lover or a psychiatrist, who might bring up among her confidences that old story. Too clever, you say? Then we were too clever before she ever came. And yet," he brooded, "it was logical to take a fall and make a reason for Fox's scar. Which the Neppers saw. And although they are gone, Moon saw it. Sarah must never see it. Sarah must not be put in mind of scars."

Malvina wrung her hands. "Be cross," she said. "It would be easy."

The old man sent her a look of disdain and then he sighed. "Did you test this man?" he asked thoughtfully.

"Never been to England," Malvina said shortly. "Not interested in theatrical people."

"Well, then, I shall see him. I think . . . yes . . . we will have him here."

"Here!"

"For a witness," said the old man, whose true name was Arthur Lupino.

"A witness, Grandfather?" said Malvina in her throat. Her face became smooth and serene as if she put the mask snugly on.

"He persists, does he? This David Wakeley?" said the man known as Fox. "Why, don't you see? That's torn it." He had a coquettish way of turning his head and there were deep dimples around his mouth. He rolled his dark eyes that were still roguish. "It's only Sarah," he said soothingly. "Only Sarah who would know the mark. Only Sarah who could claim the property. Without Sarah . . ." He spoke as if he wished her

39

to agree to remodel the house. "Now, Malvina, you know you are tired of it."

"I know, Grandfather," said Malvina.

"Now, then," said Fox and his eyes turned, the pupils sweeping over and down as if he glanced inward, "I will make a plan and you must do as I say."

# Chapter 4

Sarah sat on the sand. A more isolated spot
could scarcely be imagined. Tide was in: there
remained no more than a few square yards of
beach. Therefore, close behind her rose the
precipitous promontory at whose base, on her left,
were tumbled rocks, no thoroughfare. To her
right, a huge boulder made a barrier between her
and the inward sweep of the coastline. The
existence of this tiny cove was not apparent from
the other side of the rock. No one, as far as Sarah
knew, had ever scaled it or waded around it to
intrude upon this most private and most lonely
place.

She had come down the zigzag path from the
shelf to dip briefly and sun herself, but she must
soon climb back again because the afternoon was
getting chilly. The night would be cool. But she
sat on, with her short terry-cloth beach robe drawn
around her bare shoulders, staring out to sea. Birds
came and went about their business. Against the
sea's crashing, the bird-cries or some sudden bustle
of wings in a take-off were the only sounds.

Sarah made no sound and she did not move

except to shiver and she did not shiver altogether because of the cold.

School was over and summer had come in. She would not see David Wakeley for a long time, if ever again. Nor would she, probably, have news of him. Right now, she didn't even know that he was safe. For all she knew, something might have already happened to him . . . as it had happened to all the others.

She was tormented by this ignorance and afraid to try to find out whether he was safe. His image haunted her. She knew him so well, having watched and listened to him three hours every week for an entire term. She knew his voice, his ways of speech. She knew his mind, its warmth and vivacity. She knew his gestures, that tuft of hair at his crown that wanted to stand up, the smooth passage of his left hand over it from time to time. She knew how the hand went down and remained upon the back of his neck, while his face wore that rueful look it had when he was puzzled. She knew the earnest pull of his brows when he was intent, and the sunrise effect of his smile. She knew it could electrify fifteen female hearts in that classroom.

Whispers blew by her. She had seen the blush, or the pretty ankle well displayed. She had watched the swaying walks up to his desk after the lecture, the young faces yearning up . . . almost heard the hearts throbbing. To have a crush on Wakeley was as routine as vaccination. For a girl, it was almost a part of the course.

Yet, boys and girls together, he stung them all to mental exercise beyond their original intentions. He knew how to deflate the show-offs and encourage the shy. He was a good teacher. He will

42

write a good book, she thought.

A bird cried: the lonely protest of the sound echoed in Sarah's breast. It had hurt a great deal to say no. She thought she would rather help David Wakeley write his book than travel around the world, than be crowned Queen, than find the treasure of the Incas, than discover a new thing like radium, than win the Nobel prize . . . than any foolish dream that had ever gamboled through her mind.

Sarah was twenty-eight years old. Once upon a time she had been in the stream of life, working, playing, flirting, fighting. But now she did not dare. There was one thing more. *Her* heart was no giddy young heart. It would not, like the other fourteen in the classroom, so easily forget him and pass on.

Sarah's hair fell around her ears and her head went down. Or forget his sweetness, his respectful listening, his stubborn sympathy. Her thoughts circled wearily. Forget him, she thought, because there is nothing I can do. Couldn't work close beside him, not while this strange and evil thing hung over her. Would it ever lift?

Well, she had been in love with Peter Lamont and he was dead and she had never known him and he was beginning to be forgotten. So it was possible to forget, to leave love out. But was it possible to leave life out, friends, work, human connections? She thought it was not . . . not much longer.

Sarah threw off her brooding, brought herself into that control that was being exercised a little too often these days. Better go up now. Dress and join them in the big room by the fire and listen to Grandfather talking before dinner. It was too lonely here. It was too lonely everywhere.

She put on her rubber-soled shoes and thrust her arms into the coat sleeves. Found her glasses and put them on. She began to climb. The path was narrow. It went looping back and forth but steadily upward. It never leveled off, so that the climb although not steep was long and breathtaking. From the top Sarah could see the ugly rocks straight below. She shivered in the sea-borne breeze.

Gust Monteeth, the manservant, kept a tub of clear water here beside the glass door at the end of the bedroom wing. Sarah carefully washed her feet of sand and dried them on her towel. Shoes in her hand, she let herself in at the end of the long corridor.

On her left were two bedrooms, her own first, then Malvina's. On the right the door to Grandfather's bedroom from which enormous chamber he had access to his hexagonal study at the front of the house. But the passage in which she stood led straight through to the living room and, looking along it now, Sarah thought for a moment that she was hallucinating.

She could see firelight on a face, the face of a man who was sitting, quiet, established, big as life, in a chair at Grandfather's fireside. She thought the man was David Wakeley. Sarah leaned on the wall and closed her eyes. Then there was something wrong with her. Maybe it was true, what she so often felt was implied in Malvina's smile, in Edgar's taciturnity. Much, that she thought she knew, was illusion.

She could hear Grandfather's voice. "I try not to speak too often or too boastfully of the old days," he was saying in his chirruping way, "It makes me feel old, you see. But we were clever. Yes, we were. And my dear old Lupino, *he* was the cleverer of the two of us."

After a little silence a man's voice said, "Have you any film records, sir?"

Sarah could have sworn it was David Wakeley's voice . . . his known familiar voice. Her heart began to pound and the shoes fell out of her hand.

"Is that Sarah? Tell Sarah to come here," said Grandfather.

So she opened her eyes and Malvina was coming toward her. "Grandfather wants you, Sarah. Come along in." Malvina's voice was gentle as if she spoke to an unhappy child.

"I can't come," said Sarah. "I must dress."

"Grandfather wants you to come in now, because Mr. Wakeley must leave soon." There was not the slightest hint in Malvina's manner that Sarah had said anything worth attention.

Sarah's mouth was dry as a bone. She walked on her cold bare feet upon the bristly carpet. She came into the big room and both tall men, Edgar and David Wakeley, rose.

"Come here to me," said Grandfather from his own place on the cushioned bench of the inglenook. "Your hands are cold, little Sarah. So cold. Come, sit between me and the fire and you shall have a muffin and some tea." She must obey as if she were a child who needed coddling.

Here sat Edgar, David himself, in their town clothing, and Grandfather in his snug double-breasted deep-red velvet jacket. Malvina in her soft green gown and her golden beads. All decorously like gentlemen and a lady around the genteel tea table. And even Mrs. Monteeth, bustling in with fresh muffins, was wearing her decent black-and-

45

white. But here Sarah must come in a red bathing suit and a dampish white coat that came only to her knees, barefoot, with her hair sea-blown. She sat down, bewildered, in the chimney corner.

David sat down again quite near Malvina.

"We have made plots," said Grandfather roguishly, "while you have been gone. Now, I won't tell you until you are cozy and warm."

"Tea, Sarah?" asked Malvina.

"Put a drop of rum in it," said Edgar without emotion. "She looks frozen."

"If you had let me dress . . ." said Sarah struggling against an atmosphere of pity and indulgence.

"Now, it doesn't matter," cried Grandfather. "She looks very charming, eh Mr. Wakeley?" His bright eyes peered at David.

"But hardly businesslike," said David, "or secretarial."

Sarah's heart jumped into her throat and she wanted to cry out, No, don't . . . But of course one never did anything to startle Grandfather. One must do as he wished and move only gently.

"Do you like the muffins?" asked Grandfather, licking butter from his thumb. "Moon does something extraordinary to them. My Chinese cook, Mr. Wakeley. Not one word he says is comprehensible to us. But he understands what *we* say, although somewhat adventurously."

Sarah had heard Grandfather talk about Moon before. She drank tea with rum in it, desperately bewildered, while Grandfather, nodding and dimpling and using his short-fingered plump hands in punctuating gestures, explained about Moon. How he always got a menu almost exactly right. But never quite. Always some little surprise, a twist of his own. "It's rather fun," said Grandfather.

"These are delicious," David said. "But I asked you a moment ago . . . I know so little about the work you did sir. I have missed a lot. Is there a film record of your . . . what would you call it . . . performances? If so I would . . ."

"Alas," said Grandfather, "no film record can catch a thing which exists only at the moment of perfect rapport between the comedian and his audience. Everything we did, Mr. Wakeley, bounced upon our audience and returned to inspire us to send back a little more. It was like tennis. But a film would be as if we hit our ball against a deadening wall. No, we were not on the films. I do not regret it."

"My loss, nevertheless," said David politely.

"You are quite right, of course," said Grandfather complacently. "The photographs give nothing."

The familiar photographs were lying, Sarah saw, by David's hand. Two little men, drowned in too much cloth, the clown-masks of their made-up faces, putty noses, charcoaled brows, both solemn, full-face toward the cameras. The photographs of Fox and Lupino had never seemed funny, but old-fashioned and grotesque, and even somewhat pathetic by their stillness as if there must have been some noise and energy about the two quaint little figures not captured in the picture and so lost forever.

"Nothing at all," said Grandfather.

David stirred. "I must think about going. I can't stay, I'm afraid." David looked at Sarah.

"Then we must explain to Sarah." Grandfather turned and took her hand. His eyes peered

47

earnestly into her face. "Mr. Wakeley, who prefers not to be called Professor . . . eh, Sarah? . . ." Sarah had a sense of coming dismay and waited helplessly. "Mr. Wakeley, then, proposes to write a history book. Malvina has taken him to see the studio over the garage and he declares it is perfect. So he will write his book here, at the Nest. And you will be his secretary."

"But I can't . . ." said Sarah faintly.

"Why, you can," Grandfather said, cocking his head with all his dimples playing. "Mr. Wakeley thinks you would like to." Sarah knew the longing and the pain were in her eyes for Grandfather to see. "It will do you so much good to be occupied, as we all agree. And there is no need to worry at all, dearie. You are safe from this bother of yours . . . you know that . . . here, with the family."

Sarah brought her trembling hands together.

"Mr. Wakeley . . . although I think I will soon come to call him David . . ." Somewhere in the blur Sarah knew that David smiled . . . "David, then," Grandfather went on, "will stay in the guest house with Edgar, and I shall have the pleasure of presiding over the writing of a book. Now fancy! Here in my Nest, to hatch such a thing! Eh, Sarah?"

"Oh, Grandfather, I . . . don't know. . . ."

"But I have seen to it," Grandfather said, the smallest hint of petulance in his voice. Sarah heard the voices joining in to explain, all the coaxing cajoling voices. And Grandfather saying, finally, "Therefore David will become a part of the family and that answers everything. Isn't it simple? Am I not clever?"

"You are so good." Sarah smiled at him. But she

48

was struggling for her identity as a grown person, against all this coaxing and petting of a reluctant baby. "Does Mr. Wakeley really want . . . ?"

Mr. Wakeley said, as if she were grown, "I can't tell you what the offer means to me, Miss Shepherd. Such a place to work is beyond anything *I* could afford. But there is no question of coming at all unless you agree. I would be delighted to come and to have your help, but you must be the one to decide whether you want to work with me."

"Surely you see what a happy plot it *is*, Sarah!" cried Grandfather.

Sarah swallowed. One mustn't thwart Grandfather too far. She sat as straight as she could. She began to feel her outcast state, for here sat four people, intelligent, grown, living people, and only she, bedraggled in the corner, was afraid of anything. "None of you," she said slowly, "none of you think there is anything to be afraid of?"

Grandfather said, "Ah, now, Sarah . . ." His dry old hand was fluttering on her own. "The ghosts can't follow you here, my dearie." Malvina was smiling. Sarah knew the quality of that smile, so fresh and kind and yet hinting scorn. Edgar's face was smooth, his small eyes watchful. He said nothing. Sarah looked searchingly at David Wakeley.

"Of course there is nothing to be afraid of," he said.

She drew in her breath, disappointed. Well, then, they had talked to him, they'd got around him, they'd changed his mind. He had said it wasn't chance. Now he must think, as Edgar and Malvina did, that most of it was moonshine.

"None of you? Only me."

"Oh, Sarah," said Malvina, her voice mournful with reproach, "Grandfather *wants* him to write his book here. And he'd *like* to. Do you never think of other people?"

"Perhaps . . ." David began and Sarah caught on *his* face that look of pity.

Grandfather interrupted. "But I have arranged it."

"I am foolish," said Sarah, stung, hurt. "And you are very good to me, Grandfather. Of course, it's a wonderful plot."

"Now, then," said Grandfather merrily. "Now, that's better. Now, he must fetch his things. I daresay he will need pencil and paper. Oh, and a typewriter. Eh, Malvina? Have we a typewriter?"

"There's the portable, Grandfather, but I imagine . . ." Malvina's glistening eyes turned to David.

"I'll bring a typewriter," David said and he smiled at Malvina as if they two were in the know about these things. "You suggested Monday, sir?"

"Monday is the day for new beginnings," chirped Grandfather. "I am so pleased to have thought of this. . . ."

Things were going too fast for Sarah. "But Grandfather, won't it . . . mightn't it disturb you? Maybe Mr. Wakeley doesn't understand . . ."

"He has been told about your grandfather's health," said Edgar in his flat voice.

"Now, how can it disturb me?" Grandfather was gay. "He will not be in the house. You and he will work quietly . . . although I confess I don't see whatever he will put in his book. But no matter, we can dine together from time to time and speak of a variety of things, I'm sure. And besides, dear Sarah, it is all for your sake."

Grandfather twitched.

And it wasn't good for him to twitch. So Sarah pumped gratitude and ease into her voice. "You are so good, it was so clever of you." She caressed his hand. "It was just the surprise . . ."

"Poor Sarah's at a disadvantage," drawled Malvina. "By Monday, dressed for the part, she will seem more efficient." Malvina's apology for Sarah succeeded in pointing out her bare feet, her wild hair, her doubt and her quaking.

"I hope I will be able to hang on to *my* efficiency," David said, "in this beautiful place." His eyes were on Malvina as he rose.

He was perceptive enough not to weary Grandfather with many thanks or too much leave-taking. He said, "Walk with me to the gate, Miss Shepherd?"

"We all will," said Malvina charmingly.


So Malvina walked beside him across the garden, purring like a great cat, a big comfortable domestic pussycat, talking about the routine of the house and, like a cat, she seemed to be arching her back and puffing out her fur.

Sarah's bare feet stumbled and were bruised on the bricks. "Edgar," she appealed, "I don't know . . . I don't like this. . . ."

"If your grandfather says it's all right . . ." murmured Edgar. He was watching the two who walked ahead.

"Malvina," Sarah caught at her sleeve, "please. Stop, all of you. Please. Mr. Wakeley, don't you see, if anything should happen, how I would feel?"

"Oh, Sarah, not that again," Malvina said in a

soft wail that was sorry and disgusted, and bored with her, too.

The garden was growing dark but light fell on the flowers that curtained the cliff and on David's face. He was not smiling. He was looking down at her rather intently. "I really don't think you must let this thing get you down," he said. "Let's be sensible. After all, we know things don't just happen." His eyes held hers. "Now, do they?" He took her hand.

Sarah said helplessly, "I'll try . . ."

"Then, I'll see you on Monday."

"We'll look forward . . ." said Malvina charmingly. She went to unlock the gate and David took her hand to say goodbye. He walked away toward a smart red car.

Sarah stood at the top of the stairs and even in her strange state, part a quenchless feeling of joyous excitement, and part dismay, she thought to herself, Why, that's not his car.

But Malvina turned and began to come up and Sarah turned to run away. That first day she had come here and found Grandfather, she had felt easy and at home after some long terrible weeks. Until Malvina had come, storming and scolding, and making it clear that Sarah might have killed the dear old man with such a shock. Malvina had even discharged the couple . . . the Neppers . . . because Mrs. Nepper, in all kindness, had let her in. Sarah had never thought it was fair, never quite liked Malvina Lupino. Never trusted her temper.

She felt Edgar take hold of her shoulders and give her a little push. "Go, get dressed," he said. "This hasn't got anything to do with you. If *Malvina* wants him here," said Edgar bitterly, "he'll come."

Sarah began to hurry across the garden. She looked back. Edgar was looking thunderous. Malvina was smiling her wide frank smile and her eyes were lifted, wide and innocent, to his scrutiny.

Sarah, trying to banish misgivings and forebodings, trying to be sensible, could not banish the one deep joyous cry. It has to do with me. I will be working by his side.

A few miles away, the other side of the settlement, David sat on the floor beside Consuelo's fire, eating his supper quickly off a divided plate. "So you didn't mention me at all?" she mused.

"Thought I'd better not. After, Consuelo, you weren't let in. Besides, I want you working in the dark. You are my secret service."

"I'm a genius at it, too," said Consuelo smugly. "Never knew my own resources. For instance, I can tell you a lot about Edgar Perrott."

"Pray do," said David with his mouth full.

Consuelo, who was supping from a tray, put her fork down. "He is some distant connection of Fox's. He hails from Fresno. I got on the phone. Seems this Edgar got into a jam. He either did, or was only suspected of doing, what no ethical doctor would do. And while he got off with a verdict of 'not proven,' his practice fell out from under him. So Edgar was down and out and very low, some four or five years ago, when he approached the Fox. Now, I imagine he is up there for two reasons. One, I think he's lazy and Fox keeps him. Two, his reputation has that spot on it."

"Three," said David, "he is wild for Malvina

and as green-eyed as they come."

"Imagine!" sighed Consuelo. "And is Malvina wild for him?"

David cast her a worried glance. "What about the money? Did you find out anything?"

"Sure. I found out that if you are brash enough you can intimidate respectable people into telling you a heck of a lot more than they should. I pumped young Gordon. Fox is in the chips, all right. Willed it, share and share alike, to those girls."

"Don't tell me. Let me tell you," groaned David. "When one girls dies without an heir . . ."

"Wrong!" said Consuelo. "Survivor does *not* take all. Fox is too smart to set up anything like that."

"Then I can't see . . ."

"Neither can I. And there's this, too, Davey. Sarah gets a modest allowance, right now, but Malvina gets a good-sized amount on the excuse that she is Fox's right-hand woman and earns it. Looks as if Malvina has no money motive whatsoever but to count her blessings. And look at their attitude. You say they seem to worry about Sarah, say they seem to want to help her, ask you right in there just to give Sarah a job and keep her happy. Sounds to me," said Consuelo dejectedly, "as if we are fresh out of villains. Edgar may not always have been the most upright soul in the world, but what on earth motive would he have to harass the girl? Malvina, who rattled around with some pretty scummy people when she was young, may or may not be a reformed character, but she is sitting pretty. As for Fox, he seems to have been the noble benefactor all around."

David's hand was massaging the back of his

neck. "Well, I dunno," said he.

"You don't!" cried Consuelo with delight. "Tell me."

"One little thing . . ."

"Go on. Go on."

"Listen carefully while I quote."

"I'm falling out of my chair listening, you great goop."

"When I put it to Fox that I wanted Sarah to work for me, this is what he said." David began to mimic the old man's voice. " 'I do appreciate your interest and your courage, too, Mr. Wakeley. You are not frightened? The accident doesn't . . .' " David stopped and looked up at her. "Right there, Malvina breaks in and says quickly, 'Of course Sarah's little accidents don't frighten Mr. Wakeley, Grandfather. Mr. Wakeley is a reasonable man.' So then Fox says, 'Perhaps you would be very good for our poor Sarah. Yes. Yes, I do think so.' "

David's mimicking voice ceased.

"Accident . . ." said Consuelo thoughtfully.

"*The* accident. Not plural."

"What?"

"Now, Consuelo, I have heard many people say 'He don't' incorrectly. But I've never heard one say 'They doesn't.' Fox was talking about *one* accident. And what accident? Mine. I'm certain that Fox knows about my car."

Consuelo felt a goose go over her grave.

"How does he know? I didn't tell anyone, especially not Malvina. I think there must have been some slip. He *thought* I had told Malvina."

"And she tried to cover up that slip!" Consuelo's soft old face looked as ferocious as possible.

"And therefore Malvina also knows. And moreover, the old man let her cover and he went along

55

with that. And if they *do* know about my car and *don't* speak of it to me, then there sure is something devious and dishonest going on."

Consuelo said uneasily in a moment, "Do you think you'd better go and stay there? Possibly it's a nest of snakes, Davey."

"That's why I jumped at it," David said. "One thing worries me. I'm on a false basis with Sarah. Couldn't speak to her aside, you know. There wasn't a chance. I'll have to make one. She doesn't realize why I'll be there."

"Davey, you'll get no work done."

"I don't expect to. Don't plan to try."

"They may try . . . to fix another piece of bad luck up for you."

"How I hope they do!" he said. "I can hardly wait."

# Chapter 5

The Monday was one of those glorious days
when the whole world looked freshly painted in
the crystal air. For once, the ocean was properly
aquamarine. The crisp ruffles of surf, whiter than
white. The sky as blue as a back-drop.

The red car flashed up the road at ten exactly.
David walked into a burst of welcome. Gust
Monteeth, a bent and durable-looking man,
respectfully carried his bags into the guest house,
which stood apart, backed up against the bluff at
the land side of the garden. Edgar was there, like a
sub-host, showing him his half of the cottage.
Then he was introduced to Mrs. Monteeth, elderly
and shapeless, with soft flabby cheeks, a flying eye,
and upright but absent-minded air. Moon was
summoned from the kitchen, an ageless Chinaman who uttered a sequence of syllables that were
gibberish to David's ear. His manner conveyed
welcome. Finally Fox himself came out into the
garden and chirruped and twinkled at him.

Malvina, mistress of all these ceremonies,
looking rather regal in a white cotton sun-dress
that might have been a ball gown, now led him to

the studio.

And there waiting, in a sedate blue cotton waist and skirt, looking very small and tense and determined, was Sarah Shepherd.

David took over. He sent Gust to carry up his books and boxes.

The garage building began from a lower level than the garden so that the studio could be entered without climbing either up or down. One passed first through a cluttered anteroom where Gust kept garden tools on one side and his saw and hammers, paint pots and plumbing aids on the other. The studio itself took up two thirds of the space of this second story and looked out upon the road, the cove, and of course the ever-present sea. There was here a big desk, a table for Sarah, many shelves, some cushioned window benches, a chair or two, and a couch against the partition. There began a great unpacking.

David took notebooks and papers from his boxes. He had along an early draft of his first three chapters and, for the rest, he had snatched some old stuff. Now he directed Sarah firmly because he soon saw that this helped her. Occupied with classifying in her own mind the papers as he arranged them, trying to understand his system, she forgot to be frightened. David, meanwhile, kept up a running conversation with Malvina, who had sat down on one of the window benches and remained as if she were too fascinated to move.

She listened, but her interest was policy, her questions betrayed the poverty of her outlook. David could feel the little girl's swift understanding running ahead of the heavy work it was to expound upon the history of California, as he saw it, to Malvina Lupino. The big girl was all pose, all polish, all this curious, fresh and yet reticent personality of hers. David began to suspect she was wearing a mask over nothing, that the secret of Malvina was a certain numbness and stupidity.

But Sarah was as quick as his own hand.

Putting books on shelves, Sarah must have caught a glimpse through the window of the red presence on the parking apron. "Such a beautiful new car!" She spoke impulsively. And again David noticed the sheen and the sparkle that fell away when she wasn't solemn or frightened.

"Pretty flashy for a college professor," he said casually and turned to catch Malvina's expression.

She had none. She offered him her blinkless gaze. "I hope the salt air won't be too bad for it," Malvina purred. "We can't offer you garage space unless we share off. Sarah's little Chevy stands out, as it is. There's Grandfather's Cadillac, and Edgar's Dodge, and my convertible. Even so, we haven't enough cars. Moon, going to market today, had to borrow mine."

"It's a fantastic world," David said, shaking his head, "where nobody walks. Here's what I was looking for, Miss Lupino."

"Malvina," she corrected, lips parted.

"Now that is a direct quotation from the Spanish . . ."

Malvina looked at the page and blinked.

"My handwriting," groaned David, "I know. It's terrible. Sarah?"

"Yes, sir."

"We may as well know the worst. Can *you* read my handwriting?"

"Of course I can." He saw the flash of emotion cross her face. She took the paper and read off fluently what he had written on it.

59

"You can. Well, good. That will save work." He twitched the paper out of her hand and went on talking to Malvina.

But he remembered and realized he had omitted to consider a thing he had once divined. This girl . . . Now he remembered the two betraying words she had said to him in that cafeteria. *"Not you,"* she had said. This girl—he groaned to himself, feeling sorry—was fond of him. David was used to it in all those young students. He wished it were not so of Sarah. This was a factor he wished he did not have to deal with. He was sorry.

When Edgar put his head in and announced that lunch was ready in the garden, Malvina professed to be surprised. "Where has the morning gone? We have been spellbound!"

"Heard the lecture myself," said Edgar dryly. "Down in my lab. It came very loud and clear right through the floor."

David passed his hand over his hair. "Look here, am I going to disturb you? I'll have to be doing a lot of dictation and the typewriting will go on and on."

"I don't mind. If you don't," Edgar said. He had a small mouth under a long upper lip. When he tried to clamp his mouth sourly it merely looked childish. "Lunch," he repeated. The small eyes were fixed upon Malvina.

As they left the studio, Edgar pointed out the gap in the wall between garage and kitchen wing where a flight of steps went down to his own little cubby-hole built against the lower story of the garage proper. Edgar explained that he fooled around in there intermittently. He seemed vague about it. They passed Moon's ridiculous little kitchen garden. They came to the round table set

60

under the carob tree.

David looked around. "Miss Lupino . . . Malvina . . . this will not do. Please, after today, could Sarah and I have a sandwich or something in the studio? I'll never get any work done otherwise."

"No need to be social that I can see," said Edgar gloomily.

"After today," Malvina's soft promise went to David, or Edgar, or both . . . there was no telling.

David felt some relief when Malvina excused herself after lunch. Fox had not appeared. He was somewhere within and apart.

Edgar, however, almost as if he had been instructed, did not leave them until they came to the steps that went down. Then, still with that air of obedience, he swung off to go to his lab again. David bit his lip and reflected. So, Edgar could hear through the floor, could he? David was trying to phrase something to say to her, quickly, as they went through the toolroom, when Sarah turned to him.

"I hope, I pray, that all of you are right, and that I am wrong to be so jittery. After all that's already happened, I can't help thinking of it."

David made a gesture trying to warn her about Edgar, somewhere too near. But he was seeing, and wishing that he could not see, how the small face was betraying the heart again.

"I will try not to be foolish," Sarah said proudly. "I'll enjoy the work very much, I know."

David was touched by the little speech, by her rather tremulous smile. And then they were in the studio already. So he said, rather coolly, remembering Edgar, "I think if we stick to a businesslike job of work there is nothing to be jittery about." It was cool enough to hurt a little, he could tell. "If you really can read my handwriting," he continued swiftly, "do you mind typing off these quotations while I do some necessary pondering?" He showed her the form he wanted.

She went to her table. He knew his coolness was a steadying thing. So long as they worked, so long as she had enough to do, so long as he didn't let her know he'd guessed the secret . . . He sat in his chair and looked studious with his fingers in his hair. He must sooner or later say something to her about his suspicions. But he didn't want to frighten her. She was frightened enough. She'd had a rough time. She was somewhat too fond of him. He wondered how he could manage not to hurt her any more. Out of the corner of his eye he could see her typing away, slowly relaxing and falling into rhythm as a good typist must. He realized he couldn't fool her for long. She would know before the day was out that he was writing no book here.

He thought, Does Edgar want to know what we say to each other? If so why does he tell me he can overhear? There was a formless tension in this place and not all of it was coming from Sarah.


Fox was saying to Malvina, "What I ask you to do is surely very simple."

Malvina stood before him in the study, with her hands clasped. "So *soon?*" she said.

"It must be soon," he snapped. "Moon markets today which is the reason I settled on a Monday. Can't keep Edgar eavesdropping forever. He could only interrupt a dangerous trend of talk between them once or twice. Not more. No, no. I don't intend to risk them alone together more than this one hour."

Malvina said, "Grandfather, I don't understand what you are going to do."

"You don't need to understand."

"You must think of the dangers . . ."

"You have only to do what I tell you. I have arranged a most safe role for you, Malvina." His head was tilted in his old coy manner but the dark eyes were not twinkling.

"And you?" she asked.

"Oh I protect myself, of course."

"But I don't see how."

"You forget how clever I am."

"What is that?" She was watching his hands. "Is that poison, Grandfather?"

"No, it is not," snapped Fox. "I haven't any. Edgar has some." His dark eyes rolled thoughtfully. "I am aware of the dangers," he said. "Now, poison is a dangerous thing."

"But what will happen? Edgar is out there."

"Edgar," said Grandfather in a voice of contempt, "will look after himself. Anyhow, *he'll go*, if Wakeley goes. He wishes to go to the village and that was my instruction."

"He won't like hearing what I say." Her face was shrewd. She seemed certain.

"Never mind. I can control Edgar. So can you, when it is necessary. And never forget, if Edgar speaks now, he confesses he sent a car down a hill upon a woman. No, Edgar knows nothing of my plan in advance and will say nothing of it afterward, whatever he may surmise."

"You are very sure of yourself, Grandfather," she murmured.

"I stepped into Fox's boots, didn't I, when that seemed impossible? I got us out of England and not one soul saw which of us it was that left alive. Didn't I?"

"With my help, Grandfather."

"Then help me now, Malvina," the old man said impatiently.


David turned his head slowly. "I've come to tempt you!" Malvina was gay. She stood in the toolroom door wearing a black bathing suit, towels and robe hung over her arm. Her long smooth legs were beautifully shaped, her shoulders were plump and lovely. Her smile was brilliant. "This *day!* This *weather!* It's criminal not to be using it. David? You haven't even seen our little beach."

He saw Sarah's neck rigid.

"You'll have bad luck if you don't yield," teased Malvina. "Can't you see how wicked and against nature it would be? Let Sarah go on with whatever it is, and come out into the sun. Your first day? In a little while it will be too chilly. Half an hour? Even twenty minutes? Recess?"

David made a sound, half laugh and half sigh. He felt a surge of excitement. Could there be something of a plot in this? He hoped so. He was impatient. He couldn't work on his book, anyhow. "Malvina," he said, "you have ruined my afternoon."

"Oh, surely not." She was flirtatious.

"My afternoon's work," he amended smoothly. His hand batted down the lock on his crown. "You really don't need me, do you Sarah?" he asked whimsically as if she were his taskmistress.

He saw that Sarah was in panic.

"What on earth's the matter, Sarah?" said

Malvina in a voice of pure wonder that was in itself a falsehood. She must know what ailed Sarah.

David was on his feet close beside her because she looked as if she might faint. "It never helps to be afraid," he said quietly. He touched her on the shoulder and she winced as if he'd hurt her. "Don't you think it will help," he went on soothingly, "if we all try to believe that nothing bad is going to happen?"

"Nothing's going to happen," said Malvina plaintively. "Oh, dear. Sarah, you spoil everything."

"Would you like to come, too?" David's voice was kind. "And look after me?"

He was sorry he'd said it. Her face flooded with the color of shame.

"Sarah doesn't swim at all," said Malvina pityingly. "But I can look after you, I'm a very strong swimmer."

"I am a strong swimmer myself," said David. "I doubt if I'll drown. Sarah?" He didn't want to leave her in that panic. It seemed cruel.

But Sarah said stiffly, "I don't want to spoil things."

"Good girl. Wait a minute." David went to his desk and scribbled a note on a piece of paper. *Seems to me we are being watched,* he wrote. *And it looks mighty funny. I came to find out what goes on here. Must talk to you alone. Don't worry. One thing it isn't. That's ghosts.*

He slipped the paper under another on Sarah's table. "Add this, please," he said. "And don't worry." Now she looked more green than red and he added sharply, "And I'd like that stuff to go over this evening if it's possible."

"Yes, sir," said Sarah.

Malvina said, "Oh David, hurry, do. The sun will be going." She took his hand. So they went away.

Sarah sat before her typewriter, holding her head together with both hands. All the long train of her sorrows was dragging through her memory. She heard them saying, "Last to see him alive, Sarah . . . Sarah was the last to see him alive." She saw Peter whom she had loved and married and never grown to know, lying on the ground beside her wedding shoes. She felt the black evil bird flapping its wings around her head, the doom that followed where she went. She knew no reason for it. She knew it was there. Her mind had long struggled and turned and tried to get away from this knowledge, and could not. It would be the sea, she thought. Or the path, that narrow treacherous path. Or the sea. The surf against those rocks. It would be the sea or the rocks or both. David had gone with Malvina and he might never return. And Sarah the last, almost the last, to see him alive?

No, she told herself, no. Stop it. Panic must be controlled. But the studio was vast and lonely and cavernous and had no peace.

He knew what troubled her so. Why, then, had he gone? Absurd, Sarah. Absurd. A man goes swimming with a pretty woman when he's invited. He feels strong and capable. He isn't afraid of black intangibles that have no reason for being. Do your work, Sarah. But she couldn't work, she couldn't take her hands away from her head.

It had seemed good for a while, good and right

and easy, to be subordinate and left out of the conversation, helpful and quick and busy. Then, when his handwriting had been as clear to her as her own, because he was her kind of person, and they ought to have made a swift working team, able to grow closer and closer in understanding and mutual respect and liking and maybe even more . . . she had been visited with pain. *Not* so good, after all, to work beside him and never dare be anything but subordinate and quick. See him every day. Hear him talking to Malvina.

Now she thought, Malvina can have him. I will give him up altogether. Only let him be safe.

She heard Edgar slam the door of his little room below and run up the steps. In a moment she heard the iron gate clang. A car started up beneath her. She turned her head enough to see the road and it was Edgar, of course, rushing away so violently. Edgar had been able to hear Malvina's coquettish invitation and he was upset. Edgar worshipped Malvina although she encouraged him so little.

Sarah rolled her head from side to side. No use to pretend she could stand aside and give up David to Malvina. No use to pretend she herself didn't want to grow closer and closer in companionship and affection. Or dream she could. It was impossible. Could not work with David here. Or anywhere. If he came back safe again she would have to tell him so, and tell Grandfather, somehow.

Grandfather's own voice surprised her. "Ah, my poor Sarah. They have left you to do all the work and your poor head aches, too."

"Grandfather . . ."

The little man was there, looking at her with his head to one side, chirruping kindness. "Now, don't fuss about me, dearie. I've only come for a

67

trowel. Gust and I are making a little change along the sea walk." He came nearer. "Poor Sarah. You find this work too difficult?"

Sarah said, "I . . . I don't think I can do it, Grandfather. I'm sorry."

"Poor Sarah. So much trouble," he said, stroking her hair. "Ah, and your head aches, does it?"

"A little." She tried to smile for the dear old man.

"Then I've the thing for that," said he, rummaging in his pockets. "Here we are." He drew out his gold pill box. "My poor Sarah, there is no need for pain. Now, you will take a nice little pill. Perhaps two, eh? And then you will lie quite still so that they can work, you understand? And soon you will feel quite well again." She felt it pleased him to try to help her.

So, to please him, Sarah moved to the couch against the partition while he went to fetch water from a carafe.

"Lie back, dearie."

"I'm sorry, Grandfather. I'm sorry, after all your kind thoughtful plans . . ."

"Now, then, pop them down."

"You are so good to me, Grandfather. When I ought to be taking care of you."

"Come, Sarah, I'll tell you a secret. I am not so helpless as people think, eh?"

Sarah felt he was happy to be fussing over her. She thought to herself suddenly, Yes, I *will* collapse. I will break down. It went against her grain to make such a resolution, but she made it. Because then David would go away and get another girl to help him. And he would be out of reach of the incomprehensible doom that haunted her.

"You should have a coverlet," the old man fussed. "I'll send Mrs. Monteeth. Now rest, sleep. And the headache will go away, I promise you." He stroked her hair.

"So good . . ." murmured Sarah and tears came into her eyes.

She thought bitterly it would be better to escape in sleep than be waiting superstitiously for the cry, the news, the rising up of shock out of this golden day. It was difficult to focus on her panic or her resolutions either, lying there. She did began to fall away from consciousness, very swiftly indeed. For while she yet heard him moving about in the toolroom, looking for that trowel, Grandfather's pills were already putting her to sleep. Sarah let herself fall.

Fox, in the toolroom, was not looking for a trowel. He arranged the cotton waste as he wished, down between the cans of paint and varnish. He took care to slop a little varnish out of one opened can. Then he took Sarah's own cigarette lighter, held carefully so as to leave no fingerprints but her own on its metal surfaces. He lit it and, with some difficulty, for it was a breeze-proof type, he got the flame to go out. Open, then, but unlit and harmless, he dropped it among the debris.

He sighed and tipped and peered and saw Sarah's eyes closed and heard the quality of her breathing. Then he set the very small candle down among the inflammables, just so. Then he lit the candle with a match.

He went, swiftly for an old man, up the short walk to the kitchen. Moon was not there but Mrs.

Monteeth was, as he knew. "Dear ma'am," said Fox, "Sarah has fallen asleep in the studio. Take her a coverlet, please do. Quickly, quickly, because Gust and I need you at once out on the sea side."

He watched her scurry into her room off the kitchen, snatch up an afghan from her bed. Mrs. Monteeth did, always, just as she was told. She vanished into the toolroom and he stooped and rubbed his varnish-tainted hands into the soil deeply several times. Then he scooped up with those hands a small plant, roots and all. Mrs. Monteeth came out of the toolroom. Grandfather sighed deeply. He was a master of timing, this little man—given a cast of people who would obey him.

"Sound asleep," said Mrs. Monteeth, smiling her rather vacant smile. "Snorin'."

Grandfather nodded. "Poor little Sarah," he said. They walked together through his house and came out again upon the sea side of it. Gust was there, digging a narrow strip of soil along the house wall. Mrs. Monteeth took up and held obediently a string stretched tight to make a guide for Gust's spade.

"Now, this," the old man said, offering the plant. "I thought the color . . ."

"That?" said Gust. "Won't stand the wind, sir." He was used to the old man. There wasn't much sense telling him this. The old man would have the plant he wanted. No matter what anyone said. The old man always thought he was smarter and his way was right. And you didn't want to argue with him if you'd keep the job. Nobody really argued with him. Unless it was Moon. But then, nobody knew for sure what Moon was saying. Gust looked over his shoulder at the brilliance

70

behind him, where the cliff fell away as the ledge stopped. This sea walk was no more than eight feet wide.

"There *is*," said Fox with satisfaction, "quite a brisk breeze today."

Sarah turned and her breath moaned. The candle burned rapidly. Flame ate upon the waste. Smouldering, spurting, it crept toward the varnish.

Deep down on the little beach, on the far side of the headland, David sunned himself on the sand beside Malvina.

# Chapter 6

They had gone into the water to swim strongly
for only a very few minutes. The water was bitterly
cold.

Now Malvina sat passively, with an air of utter
innocence, beside him. There was no coquetry, no
purpose in her at all. Restless, David thought that
by now Sarah would have found and read the note
he had slipped on her desk. He thought it would
have braced her and brought her out of that panic.
He looked sideways at Malvina. There was nothing to be discovered from that innocent silence.
He felt restless, and uselessly here. He did not
want to stay.

"My conscience hurts me," he said flatly. "I
should be back with Sarah and the eighteenth
century."

She stirred. Almost with an effort, she paid
attention. "Why do you care about the eighteenth
century," purred Malvina, too carelessly, "or
Sarah, either?"

There was such ignorant contempt in the roll of
her brown eyes, such a complacent assumption
that by the flick of a lash she could keep him where

he was, that David was angered. He didn't let the anger show. Instead he got up in one swift motion and snatched up his towel. "Recess has been fun," he said cheerfully.

"Wait. David . . ."

But he was starting up the path.

"David!"

"Yes?"

"I wanted to talk to you," she said, "alone." Her face was tilted up, he had an odd foreshortened view of it. "Please come back."

He thought perhaps she had a purpose, after all, and he had better see what could be gleaned from it. Reluctantly, he turned to come down. As he turned, he could see a fishing boat far out on the water and he noticed some excitement, something abnormal about the way the people were behaving. He shaded his eyes. They were waving their arms, obviously they were shouting, although he couldn't hear them. And they were pointing.

Moon was driving Malvina's car through the cove when he saw the fire. He stopped the car, jumped out and ran to the nearest house. His jabber was not understood but his gestures were. The woman stepped out of her house and saw the fire and ran to the phone.

David, unable to see any cause for excitement from where he stood, began to hurry up the path. But he took it warily, wondering if this, in some way, was what he was supposed to do. He was looking for danger to himself. Was he supposed to

74

run up this unfamiliar path too fast and trip on something? Not me, he thought.

He got to the top safely and saw Fox and Gust and Mrs. Monteeth, busy as they could be, heeding nothing. He started to walk along the sea walk, which led toward Fox's study and the three of them, when he saw the streaks of smoke against the serenity of the bright blue sky. So he turned to his left and ran through the gap in the garden wall.

The near end of the garage was a wicked mass of hurtling flames. The sound of a siren broke on his ear but David kept running. He remembered that the iron gate would be locked, so he swerved and went down Edgar's steps. The laboratory door was locked. No use in that. David climbed on the steep land around the sea side of the building. The garage doors stood open, all three pairs of them. He used the nearest door for a ladder. He broke glass. He tumbled over the sill.

She was alive in there, floundering drunkenly. With her hands thrust inside his leather brief case she was beating weakly at some flaming thing on his desk. He picked her up. The brief case fell. She snatched at paper. He threw her over his shoulder like a sack. He got half over the sill and slid her body forward feet first and finally, taking her by her reddened wrists, he lowered her until her feet touched ground.

She could not stand. She fell backward and he tumbled and scrambled out after her, picked her up again, and ran across the turn-around and the parking apron, as far as he could go before the hillside stopped him. The fire truck came screaming up around the hairpin-turning road.

They drenched that dry wild hillside at once and

David sat in the mud, water trickling past him with Sarah's unconscious body across his knees while Edgar, who had come in his car on the heels of the firemen, worked over the burns on her forearms.

"How did it happen?" Edgar dithered. "How did it happen?"

"I don't know. How could it?" David snapped. "It wasn't anything in your lab?"

"No, no. See, my lab wasn't touched. The fire is all above." Edgar's eyes rolled.

"The fire is where Sarah was," said David. The doctor's face seemed to close and give nothing away. David's eye traced the bone of Sarah's brow and the curve of the cheek, which was lovely. Edgar had her glasses in his pocket. Without the big glasses she was not David's owl. She looked defenseless.

When the fire was under control he picked her up again, the small warm burden, and carried Sarah to her bedroom.

Malvina wore a yellow robe over that black bathing suit. "Is she all right?" she asked, impatient to know.

"She'll be all right." Edgar was brusque. He did not look at Malvina. "Pain in those wrists when she comes out of it. Mrs. Monteeth is going to have to stay with her. I'll tell her what to do."

"Mrs. Monteeth . . . ?"

"I want her with Sarah," snapped Edgar. "I don't want Sarah alone." He gave Malvina a quick fierce glance and his mouth made itself grim.

Then Mrs. Monteeth came into the room where a small limp Sarah lay. David stood with Malvina in the corridor as the door closed them out.

"Sarah's an heiress, I suppose," said David sharply. "Who gets her share if she should die?"

Malvina gasped. "I never thought . . . I suppose *I* would."

She spoke so fast that David believed her. He'd thrown her that brutal question and the answer had bounced back. Now she looked at him as if she were reviewing question and answer with belated concern. Well, he thought, of course Malvina would get it. The old man, alive, could make another will.

"How is your grandfather?" snapped David. "From what I've been told about his heart . . ."

"Grandfather has borne it very well," said Malvina, retreating into her mysterious serenity. "I have been with him, of course. The men said the house was safe so we kept in the study where he could not see the fire. We did our best to be very calm. We didn't speak of it."

*She* was very calm. Her eyes met his candidly, openly. But it was as if she had been standing unself-consciously foursquare, and now suddenly went into an arabesque. David rubbed his palm on his cheek and looked at the grime. "What *did* you speak of?"

"Nothing. We played Camelot."

David, filthy and grim, said rather angrily, "And who won?"

"Grandfather always wins," said Malvina, faintly frowning. "You know he is very clever. Of course, he is getting old."

What she was thinking behind those winkless open eyes he couldn't tell.

"What did you want to talk to me about?" he asked.

"I forget," said Malvina.

Mrs. Monteeth had no initiative at all. Her conscience was very strict but what it told her to do was do-as-she-was-told. When the night gave over to morning and she became aware of Sarah's return to herself, Mrs. Monteeth rose at once to call the doctor.

Sarah couldn't see very well. Yet by the quality of the light beyond her window she knew it must be morning. She was in her bed. She tried to struggle up, felt a wave of pain, and saw the fat white of the bandages covering both her forearms.

Edgar came swiftly in. "You're all right, Sarah," he said briskly. "Fire's out long ago. Garage is pretty much a wreck at this end. Your grandfather's car is ruined. Nothing happened to the house at all."

"Grandfather?" she gasped.

"Grandfather is fine. Malvina was with him. He took it well." Sarah sank back. "Those arms hurt, do they?"

"It comes and goes. Edgar, what's wrong with me? Have I been drugged?"

"Of course. I doped you up. You must have been beating at the fire with something protecting your hands. Your arms got just a lick. Doesn't seem too bad. Lucky your clothing didn't catch." He helped her up a little higher in the bed. "I want you to take it easy."

She said, "The garage . . . Then the studio?"

"A mess. Darned lucky it wasn't a lot worse." There was some anger in Edgar. "Sarah, why didn't you get out? When you saw the place on fire.

All those windows . . ." He was watching her intently. "Why didn't you just get out of there as fast as you could?"

"I would have," she said, struggling with mists. "I woke up . . . you know, Grandfather gave me some headache pills. Something exploded. There was a thing like a firecracker, a piece of flame blew right into the studio through the door. I could see fire on his desk." Her tongue was thick and her voice seemed to herself to be a croaking. "Edgar, I can't see you. I need my glasses."

In a minute Edgar popped her glasses on her face. "Freak," he said making an effort to be easy. "They stayed on while Wakeley threw you out the window."

"David Wakeley threw me out the window!"

"If he hadn't . . ." said Edgar and clamped his mouth shut. He sat down and peered at her. "What were you doing, staggering around in there? Trying to beat out the fire all by yourself?"

But Sarah was tightening and shrinking with new pain. "Did he lose all his work?" she asked. "I thought I could bring it with me . . . some of it with me when I got out. But I didn't? Did it burn? Is it gone?"

"Paper?" said Edgar. His small mouth curled. "There was that one scorched scrap we found in your hand. It can't be much use."

A piece of paper, shaped like a piece of pie, browned at the edges, was lying on Sarah's dresser.

Edgar said to her stricken face, "Now Sarah, the important thing . . . nobody was hurt but you and you not badly. You've got to be quiet a few days. You are to stay right here and see no one."

"I don't want to see anyone." A tear slid out of

79

her eye corner. "He shouldn't have had anything to do with me," she mourned. "No one should."

Edgar's shoulders twitched irritably. "Do you know how the fire happened?"

"Why, I was asleep," she said. "Dopey. I still feel dopey."

"Mrs. Monteeth is getting your breakfast. She'll feed you and stay right here. Eat what you can. Then try to sleep."

"Edgar, I've been dopey a long time."

"Not long."

"A long time," Sarah insisted. "Why does it seem so hard to remember? Why was it I could hardly stand? What was it Grandfather gave me?"

"Oh, that?" Edgar gave out a short scornful laugh. "Just the stuff he takes himself. Perhaps you had a good dose of smoke, Sarah. You're full of dope right now, of course. You probably won't ever remember clearly. There's something retroactive about these shocks."

"I went to sleep so fast . . . I was scared. . . ."

"Scared?"

Edgar's voice came from a long way off. She wasn't looking at him but at her memories. "Scared because David went to the beach. He did come back all right?"

"He's O.K. He's feeling fine."

"Oh, no. He's not feeling fine. You don't understand, do you? But I do. All the work lost . . ." She wanted to sink through the bed, through the door, even into the sea. "Edgar, he will go away now, won't he?"

"Why, I think so," Edgar said. "I think David will go away now. What could keep him here?"

"Nothing. He must go. He must go right now.

Don't let him stay or come to see me. Tell him I'm sorry. Just tell him I'm sorry . . . sorry . . ."

The word was like a water-drop, repeating. It could wear away stone.

Edgar Perrott tapped on the door to the hexagonal study and was told to enter.

The old man lay in his chair, and Malvina was there, smoking, staring out at the phenomenal view.

Edgar said, "Why did you have to do a thing like that?" His face was reddish, his small eyes fierce. "Sarah told me. I don't want to have anything to do with it. I think you must be mad."

"My dear Edgar . . ." said Grandfather mildly.

"Bad enough to cheat her for years . . . bad enough to ruin her life by pounding into her head the crazy idea she's a Jonah. You don't have to *kill* her," Edgar cried.

"Sarah isn't dead, is she?" Grandfather said.

"Pills," spat Edgar. "Drugged her, didn't you? I know what you gave her. All right, I covered that up for you because I know you've got Malvina in it some way. But no more. No more."

"You weren't too squeamish in Fresno," said Fox petulantly. "And there could be trouble over David's car."

"Don't threaten me. I tell you I'm no killer. I draw the line. I mean it. I don't care . . ."

"Edgar," said Malvina and the man's eyes snapped to her. "Please, Edgar, don't upset Grandfather."

"Him and his phony heart condition? You forget, I help him with his symptoms." The big

81

man with the small head was trembling. "Malvina, do not have any part in this. You and I have done enough of his dirty work. Helped fake that fall and pretend it caused his scar. Helped watch over Sarah . . . Helped him lie and helped him steal and helped him frighten her . . . but no more." He turned on the old man and swelled with rage. "You! I'm saying to you, *no more!* It's mad anyway. This Wakeley will go away. Now he's lost his notes and he can't write any book. He won't need any secretary. Sarah won't see him again. She told me so. The whole thing is over."

Malvina put out her cigarette and laced her fingers together.

Fox said, "David tells me he wants to sift the ruins."

"What?"

"He hopes something may have come through intact."

"Paper?" said Edgar incredulously.

"Now, how can I tell him he may not stay and try?" said Fox. "Eh?"

Edgar said, "Then listen to me for once, will you? What are you trying to kill her for? You don't need to kill the girl. Probably she doesn't even remember the thing that's got you so worried. And if she did, then what? Suppose she remembered and even suppose she found out? Do you think she's going to throw *you* out into the world without a penny? Your little Sarah?" The doctor's voice sneered. "She thinks you're a saint on earth. Don't you know she'd keep you right on here and keep you surrounded with all this . . . this luxury just the same? The poor little dope is crazy about you. She'd forgive you. You haven't a thing to worry about."

"Perhaps that is true," said Grandfather, tilting his head.

"Of course it's true." Edgar lost some of his steam. "I'm glad you can see it. You should have seen it long ago. Before this fire."

"My dear Edgar," said Grandfather. "I know nothing about this fire. You mustn't be so jumpy."

Malvina said, looking as if she were blind, "Grandfather has protected himself. But she wouldn't keep *me* on here in luxury. Or *you*, Edgar."

"Ah, Malvina, Malvina, come away with me," he begged. "We can start again somewhere. Anywhere. The money is not so much . . . Come away with me, Malvina?"

Her face changed: her hands twisted. "I couldn't leave Grandfather," she said softly. "I don't . . . think I could." But in her equivocal way, she was giving him hope.

Edgar said to Fox, "Don't. Don't. Don't try that again."

Grandfather folded his lips. "Do you know, Edgar," he said finally, "you put the problem of Sarah in quite a new light. Perhaps I have been fretting for nothing, eh?"

Edgar nodded, his face flushed with victory. "Malvina, come out into the garden?"

"In just a moment, Edgar. Wait for me there."

When the doctor had gone, Malvina looked at the old man. "When I went out this morning to view the destruction," the old man said, dreamily, "the firemen were very kind. They showed me about. You know they had to break the lock on

Edgar's little laboratory? It seems they had to be sure there was no fire in it."

Malvina said nothing.

"I have some poison," Grandfather said. He seemed to brood. "I thought I had better have some. I don't like it. I am quite aware of the danger. It seems they have ways to tell whether a person has taken poison."

Malvina brushed at her skirt. "Isn't Edgar right about Sarah?" she said in a hard voice. "As far as you are concerned?"

"That I must discover," the old man said. "Perhaps. Perhaps."

"Sarah isn't very fond of *me*," Malvina said sulkily, "but I suppose you wouldn't care."

"Now come, you don't like Sarah either. Eh, Malvina? You haven't always been kind."

"*You've* taken care to be kind," she said resentfully. "If you hadn't, she might have gone back to Japan. And there'd be no problem."

"I thought it best to be kind," said Grandfather evasively.

"You *thought*," she said meanly. "But two heads may be better than one, even if that one is yours, Grandfather. Next time, better let me understand your plans."

The old man looked at her. His jaws worked. "Why, I did not fail," he said chidingly. "*You* failed, Malvina. Your simple little part. If you had kept David Wakeley on the beach, my dear. How was it you did not? Couldn't you? I am surprised."

Malvina's face grew darker.

"Perhaps you don't find him attractive?" the old man said slyly.

84

Malvina stood up, her skirt swishing. "You're going to let him stay?" Grandfather opened his palms. "David wonders, you know. He asks questions. Asked me who gets Sarah's inheritance, if she dies."

"He asked you that? He did? Indeed?"

"He did. If he is going to stay on here," there was an air of weariness and defeat about Malvina, "won't you be forced to give it up?"

"Why, not yet," said Grandfather. "Not quite yet."

# Chapter 7

Ten o'clock that Tuesday morning, David left the ruins of the studio, washed the new black from his hands, crossed the garden, and went boldly into the house by the glass door, knowing the sweet scent of charred wood still clung to his clothes. There was no one in the big room so he swung purposefully across it and into the corridor that led to Sarah. He tapped on her door.

Edgar Perrott opened it. As soon as he saw who it was, the doctor began to close the door against him. "I'm afraid Sarah shouldn't see you," he said severely through the crack. "She'd rather not, and I doubt if it's good for her . . ."

David's feet struck roots into the carpet. "The least she can do is see me," he said loudly and brutally. "Have you mentioned to her that I saved her life?"

He heard a cry within the room.

"I . . . Yes, Sarah?" The doctor said to David, "Just a minute."

David waited, feeling grim. He was going to get in to see her and he didn't care how.

The door opened in a moment and he was

admitted. Sarah's room was charming, all done in soft greens and white, with a broad window to the sea, a narrow one to the garden. Mrs. Monteeth was busy folding bedding into a neat pile on a sofa where she must have slept the night. She went on working. The doctor showed no disposition to leave, either.

David strode toward the bed where Sarah was propped on pillows. The petal texture of her face was not marred. The big glasses rode her small nose with that effect, both absurd and charming, that always brought him the image of a quaint little owl. Her beautiful mouth was suffering.

He was wrenched with pity and said more tenderly than he had expected, "How are you, Sarah?"

She didn't even make the perfunctory answer. "Can you get it back?" she said instead. "Will it be possible to do it all over again? Your work? Was it all lost?"

She was the first one to mention his loss to him and David was momentarily staggered. Others had spoken of the Cadillac ruined, the damage in dollars, the cost of the building, even the bruised and trampled garden. But not his pieces of paper, the labor of his mind. Although he had deceived her and it was not true that his work was gone, she touched him with this understanding.

"Let's not think about that," he said rather awkwardly.

"I can't think of anything else," she said. "How long did it take you? Oh, how many years?"

"Not long," he answered cheerfully. "It's not important, Sarah. I'll go at it again soon. Not now."

"No," she said immediately. "Not now. Not

right away. Oh, I am sorry . . ."

"Let me ask you a question," he interrupted. He didn't want to talk about her sorrow. He was guilty in the matter and he couldn't explain in front of Edgar. "Just how did that fire start?" She was staring at him sadly and didn't answer. "Tell me this. Had you been smoking, Sarah? Had you been using your lighter?"

"Her lighter?" Edgar edged in. "What about her lighter?"

"The men found a lighter. Gust says it belongs to her. It was opened. Whether it burst open in the heat or whether somehow or other the flame, left burning, came in contact with cloth or paper . . ."

"Sarah?" said Edgar sharply.

The blonde head moved to deny. Someone had brushed it; the pale mass of Sarah's hair was in shining order. It went like satin back from her temples and then crested over like a miniature breaker. "I wasn't smoking," she said. "I couldn't have been. I was asleep."

"Asleep!" David was astonished.

Edgar said in a quick low voice, "She was worried, you see. Couldn't work. Psychosomatic headache, I suppose. Took a couple of headache tablets and they hit her. Imagine it was escape."

David wasn't here to listen to Edgar's theories.

"The man from the fire department wants to know about that lighter," he insisted.

"I don't know anything about it," Sarah said.

"I'll talk to them. Sarah mustn't be bothered." Edgar was didactic. "I assume they think Sarah somehow or other accidentally set the fire?"

"Something set it." David was sticking to brutal simplicity. "They'd like to know what. So would I."

"If she did groggily light a cigarette she may never remem—" began Edgar.

But Sarah cried out, "Please, don't stay here! I do thank you for pulling me out. I do. I am grateful. But don't stay here any longer." Her voice was at that breaking point.

David knew that Sarah was thinking her jinx, the evil luck that followed her, had set the fire. "Don't be silly," he scoffed.

But Sarah was in a tailspin. "I was afraid . . . afraid of something. But I never thought of that. To lose all your work is the most terrible punishment . . . breaks my heart it happened because of me. Don't you see you mustn't talk to me . . . go away . . . You see you *must* go away. . . ." She was weeping.

Edgar's hand was telling David's arm to come away.

David stood there, looking down, and he knew he had to talk to her alone and right now. Of course she piled this on top of the rest. To her it was one more accident in the same inexplicable series. But she wasn't seeing, as he could see, how the bad luck had shifted. How the victim of it was no longer only Sarah's companion, but included Sarah *herself*. He didn't trust Edgar; didn't trust anyone. He had to have a chance to talk to this girl alone. He wondered how he could get it. He thought—well, he would flatly demand it. He wondered if it would work.

Sarah bowed over, trying to stifle the sound of that heartbroken weeping. David let himself be drawn toward the door, but there he struck root. He would budge no farther.

"She's pretty upset," Edgar was muttering. "You better not stay."

"I want you to leave me alone with her," said David in a low voice. "Take Mrs. Monteeth along. Let me be alone with her."

"I can't do that," said Edgar sternly. "You can see for yourself . . . the kindest thing . . ."

"I know what I'm doing," David insisted. "Will you get out of here? I've got things to say to that girl that I am not going to say in front of an audience."

"What things?"

"Personal," said David desperately. "Private."

He saw that Edgar was startled. The soft noise of Sarah's weeping ceased. She was motionless and silent. Mrs. Monteeth had heard him, too, and she straightened from her task.

Edgar said, with a writhe of the lips, "It's hardly the moment to come a-courting."

"How do you know?" David thrust at him. (Use this. Use anything.) "Give me a chance, will you? You heard her say her heart was broken? Maybe I can fix that."

Edgar licked his mouth. There was a strange glow in his eyes. He nodded to Mrs. Monteeth and she went fluttering by. Edgar followed her out and closed the door.

Delighted, David turned toward the bed. Sarah was propped on her elbows with her helpless arms across her breast. "No," said Sarah, "no, no no . . ."

"All right. *No*," said David sharply. "Skip it. Forget it. I'm not going to ask you to marry me. I ask you to listen." He went near.

Telling Mrs. Monteeth that she must remain available, Edgar himself went swiftly through the big room to the study door. Grandfather was alone there in his lair. "Oh, Edgar?" The old man was sucking fruit.

"Where is Malvina?"

"Gone to the village for a crab for my lunch."

"You had better know. Wakeley is alone with Sarah."

Fox's face darkened. "I told you . . ."

"He wants to propose to her," said Edgar with profound satisfaction. "He asked me to leave them so that he could." Edgar turned his palms, imitating the old man. "Well? Could I refuse?"

The old man began to struggle out of his chair.

"And *that's* torn it," said Edgar, still satisfied.

"You are perfectly incompetent," fumed Grandfather. "I see I must go myself."

"Go and do what?"

"Whatever can be done," snapped Grandfather.

"Tell her? Tell her the truth? You'd be better off to tell her before she finds out through Wakeley's curiosity."

Grandfather was patting himself, feeling his vest to be buttoned securely. "It is not for you to tell me what to do," he said. His face was evil and angry. Then the old man went nipping briskly through a door and didn't bother to look back.

Edgar stood and the satisfaction drained away from his face. . . .

Between David and the little blonde there seemed to be no communication. He felt as if he were batting at a wall. She was in that emotional tailspin, obsessed with her old trouble. He could not make her hear.

"I tell you I lost nothing. Nothing important. What's going on here *is* important. Please, Sarah, try to listen." He began to pace. "Don't you realize . . . Didn't you get my note?"

She didn't react. She didn't know what he was talking about.

"Piece of paper," he prompted.

"I saved one piece of paper . . ."

"This?" David glanced at the charred fragment and dismissed it. "No, no. The note I put on your table. Didn't you have sense enough to know I wanted you to read it? Gone in the fire now, of course. And you never saw it." He bent over her. "Snap out of it, Sarah. And be quick, please. There is no such thing as a Jonah. What's the matter with your brain?"

She shuddered. "But it happens. Something always happens."

"Then somebody makes it happen." He wanted to shake her. "Don't ask me why. Help me find out why."

"I don't understand . . . I don't . . ."

"Use your brain." He felt he had to be rude. "It's stupid to lie there and shudder the way you are doing. Where's your good sense? Sarah, is there anything about the money?"

"What money?" She looked perfectly bewildered.

"Somebody doesn't want you mixed up with people. Maybe that's so you won't marry. But why? Somebody might even have wanted to get rid of you in that fire." He had to be sharp and brutal to break through the wall.

"What are you trying to say?"

"I'm talking about a real enemy, Sarah. Not a jinx. Not a ghost. And it's about time you considered . . ."

"I don't know anything about money."

"Your grandfather's money."

"I could ask Grandfather . . ." she said.

David groaned. "Don't. Don't ask anyone anything. Just listen to me while there's time. First, you are going to have to get out of this place. Let me take you . . ."

"No, no. Not you."

"There you go." He was exasperated. "Why not me? Will you stop protecting me? I'm big enough to look out for myself."

"When you've lost everything . . ."

"Don't suffer for *me*," he snapped. "I prefer to suffer for myself. Just as I came here for reasons of my own. I think I made a mistake, though, because . . ."

"A terrible mistake."

"Because now it looks as if the bad luck's turned toward *you*. Now, Sarah . . ."

"Not me," she said. "Not me. I'll be all right if you will just go away."

"I'm not going away." He glared at her. "You're not listening."

"Leave me," she begged. "Only leave me."

"I'd like to slap your pretty face," he said, exasperated.

Sarah turned up her face, all anguished. "Do then," she said, "but don't stay."

"I can't slap women who wear glasses," he said flatly in a moment. He drew away. "Well, I'm disappointed." He recognized her anguish, he even understood it, but there was no time to be patient with it. "I came here," he said sadly, "in part to help you . . ."

"Don't. Don't try," she whimpered.

And he said coldly and deliberately, *"I will not leave you."* The turbulence in the room seemed to hover and then begin to die.

Sarah said despairingly, "Why?"

David leaned over and put his fingers gently on either side of her face. "Believe there are reasons, Sarah. Reasons for everything."

She turned her head convulsively and the warm soft skin of her cheek pressed upon his hand.

"Will you?" said David.

"If I could . . ." said Sarah. "If I could . . ." But she was quieted.

Somebody tapped on the door and, without waiting, opened it.

"My dear Sarah," said Grandfather. "Ah, David. How is she, my little girl?"

# Chapter 8

David choked off anger and disappointment. He smiled at Sarah and gently he took his hands away. "Sarah is fine," he said encouragingly.

"Not too upset?" purred Grandfather, advancing in his spry step. "They tell me you were not hurt too badly, dearie. Is it true?"

"Not too badly, Grandfather." Sarah swallowed all her agitation. For this old man she could exercise control.

"There now." Grandfather sat down upon the edge of the bed. "Such big bandages," said he. "Edgar says your arms will soon heal, soon heal."

"I'm sure they will, Grandfather." The tears dried on Sarah's face but she couldn't see very well through the blur they'd made of her glasses. Behind the old man's back, David wandered in the room. Grandfather's cooing voice went on and the girl seemed to have crept within some shelter where she was calm. David was not calm. He was suspicious. Just as he might have been able to talk to her, along came the old man. He heard her say, as she seemed always to be saying, "You are so good, Grandfather." He wanted to make faces, and

97

motion to her behind the old man's back. But she did not look his way. She couldn't see. And how could he, with only gestures, break into the place where she felt safe, to tell her that this old man, who was to her a refuge, might be her enemy?

But there was Edgar at the door, with Mrs. Monteeth again.

"Too many people," Edgar said. "Entirely too much company." His little eyes hunted on David's face. "I want the patient quiet. With only the nurse, please. She must not talk anymore."

Grandfather said childingly, "Now, I can comfort this child, Edgar. You know that." The old man peered around. "You don't want David? Eh, Sarah?"

"No," she said. "No."

Fox said petulantly, "Then he should go."

Edgar warned, "No scene. His heart . . ." Edgar's hand pulled steadily.

"So long," said David. He kept anger out of his voice. But it was stubborn.

Sarah said faintly, "Goodbye."

"So long," he insisted. "See you later."

He saw her teeth tear at her lower lip and he thought, A pity to tear it. Then the mouth surrendered. "So long," it said.

Mrs. Monteeth was establishing herself in the room. David thought, Well, they can't murder the girl in front of a witness. He let Edgar's pull swing him away.

Edgar, half out the door as if he would like to pursue David, warned over his shoulder, "You mustn't talk too long. For either of your sakes."

"Now, I do want to visit with Sarah a little bit," said Grandfather plaintively. "May I not? We will talk about old times, perhaps."

Edgar's eyes flickered. He said, "Not too long. Mrs. Monteeth, watch out for Sarah." Then he left the room.

He hurried, hunting David.

David was in the big room, hands in his pockets, staring at the carpet.

"Well? Is Sarah going to marry you?" said Edgar. "Or didn't you ask?" His little eyes were anxious and suspicious.

David shrugged. "I don't discourage easily."

Edgar's face changed and became nervous and desperate. "Listen Wakeley, why don't you go away from here? All you do is upset her. She's miserable enough . . . If you care anything . . ."

"I know what upsets her. I don't happen to believe in junk like Jonahs and jinxes."

"Sarah does."

"Then Sarah must learn better."

"Who are you to say?" Edgar was getting angry. "You think it's smart to be stubborn. Did it ever occur to you . . . ?" Edgar licked his lip.

"What?"

"*You* might be bad luck for Sarah?"

"What do you mean by that?" David's gaze bored into the doctor's eyes and they evaded.

"I'm trying . . . I'm trying to keep things on an even keel in this house," said Edgar in a high nervous voice. "I'm responsible for Mr. Fox's health and for Sarah's and I've got to have co-operation. If you'd just realize you're making a nuisance of yourself. Let me . . . let me *handle* this. You don't know what you are doing. I'm telling you, it's best for everyone if you go away."

"I'm sure it would be best for someone," said David, "but not necessarily Sarah."

"Yes. *Sarah*," said Edgar. "Believe me." But his

99

concentration broke. His head lifted. His ears seemed to prick up. He said, "Malvina?"

She was entering the house, stripping gloves off her hands. "May I see you a minute, Edgar?" she said coaxingly, mysteriously.

David said, "Excuse me," but Edgar didn't hear it. Malvina seemed to pay no attention either as he went by them, out of the house.

"Now, then," said Grandfather, "tears, Sarah? Why were you crying?"

"I feel so bad about David's work lost . . ."

"Work? But he can't have done much in one morning."

"All his notes, Grandfather. He must have been collecting them for months."

"Is that so?" said Grandfather. "Months, really? Well now, surely David doesn't blame *you*, does he? David is fond of you, I think." She looked as if she'd cry. "And you are fond of David, Sarah?"

Her head rolled. "I don't dare be fond of anyone."

"Not fond of *me?*" he said archly.

"Only you. I don't bring *you* bad luck, do I, Grandfather?"

"My dear little Sarah. I have outgrown bad luck, I think. I am ancient and invulnerable." Fox glanced at Mrs. Monteeth, who had placed herself in a chair and produced some knitting. She looked patient and immovable and quite detached. "But we mustn't speak about dreadful things, fire and loss and bad luck," said Grandfather, "when it makes you unhappy. Tell me, Sarah, do you remember England?"

"Yes."

"Do you remember when your mother first brought you to see me? What a little girl you were then, eh?"

"I remember." Her head turned on the pillow. Her lashes had come down. More than half her thought was on David, still. Grandfather's voice went on.

"Do you remember going to the theatre to see my dear old Lupino and me?"

"Not very well," she said. "I must have been too small."

"You didn't go many times."

"Only once, I think."

"Well, you were small. What would my dear old Lupino think, I wonder, if he could see me as I am? Here on this fabulous western edge of the world."

"If he hadn't died you wouldn't have come here, Grandfather," she murmured.

"No, that's true, dearie. True. Do you remember a week end in the country?"

"Will I ever forget it?" Sarah said wearily.

The old man peered shrewdly at her. She seemed breathless.

"The awful business," Sarah's eyes popped open, "don't you remember? About the arrow?"

"Oh, my poor Sarah, fancy your being able to remember that. Are you thirsty, dearie? I see your lips are very dry. Mrs. Monteeth, please fetch a glass of my cider. Sarah would like that."

"Doctor told me to stay, sir." Mrs. Monteeth looked lost.

"Go, *ask* the doctor, then," said Grandfather, as if this were obviously the only reasonable course, and Mrs. Monteeth accepted it, rose, and went.

"The arrow. Yes," sighed Grandfather, now that they were alone. "And dear Lupino, so brave

101

about it. So uncomplaining. Wasn't he?" He peered at the girl.

"He wasn't so . . ."

"Eh? Sarah?"

"Oh, I suppose he was brave."

"I often wish he were alive," sighed Grandfather. "Don't you, dearie? And have him here with me."

"I'm just as glad he isn't here with you," she said. "I know how you loved him, Grandfather. But to me he was . . . not so lovable."

"No?"

"No. He was cruel, I thought."

"Cruel, dearie? How was that?"

"I don't suppose he ever told . . ."

"But my dear Sarah, what was this?"

"Sorry . . ."

"Ah, now you remember my heart," Grandfather said, "but I'll tell you something, Sarah." He lowered his voice. "When you are ancient," he confided, "you do not receive a shock as people imagine. No. Too much has happened to you already. Too many friends dead, too many wars, too many shocking things. When you are old, it is all just more of the same."

"I suppose that must be true," she said.

"Then tell me. In what way was Lupino cruel?" He smiled at her with his dimples appearing in his craggy old cheeks. His teeth were not good, what few he had.

"I never told," Sarah said, "but I think of it. I can't forgive him."

"Forgive Lupino? But Sarah, my dearie, surely it was for him to forgive you."

"I never meant to hurt him with the arrow," Sarah said. *"He* was grown up. He should have known that. But one day . . ."

"Go on."

"Why, we were ready to sail for home. We went to say goodbye. He took me alone. He opened his shirt, Grandfather, and he made me look at that horrible scar and touch it. And he said to me, 'See your pretty work, young Sarah? Don't ever forget your work that you did.' Grandfather, it frightened me so. I dreamed of it. Even now, when I am unhappy, sometimes in a nightmare I can see the shape of the awful scar. To me it is the shape of a sin. But it wasn't *my* sin." Sarah said, "Oh, I'm sorry, Grandfather. I can't help thinking he was wicked and cruel to do such a thing to so small a child. I know you loved him. But that . . . that wasn't kind."

"No." Grandfather rose and drifted around the room. "Dear old chap, he was sometimes impulsive. Loved drama, you see. Oh, he grew older and wiser. He learned it was better to be kind. Yet I remember that the wound was painful and he was brave."

"Yes," said Sarah faintly. "I suppose so."

"Your David is brave," murmured Grandfather.

"He is not my . . . David doesn't believe in ghosts or jinxes."

"I think you are right," said Grandfather. "Or surely he wouldn't have come here after what happened to his car. It was a warning."

"Oh?" she said. "Yes?" And shrank on the bed.

"Rolled down the hill of itself," said Grandfather. "What an odd thing. I like the scent in this green bottle, Sarah. Of course no one blames David for what happened to the woman."

"A woman?"

The old man was quite placid, touching the

103

things on her dressing table. "Although she died," he said. "A terrible thing. Ah well, so many terrible things all over the world, happening every day. Poor woman, she was just somebody on the sidewalk. We can't grieve for everyone, dearie. Or we should never have done. Old people know that."

"David's . . . car . . ."

Grandfather drew near the bed again. "Why, it was," he said. "Such a pretty bright new one he has now, eh? Do you know he is sifting the ashes, dearie, to find if there is anything left of his? What a task! What a persistent, what a very stubborn young man he is, eh?"

Sarah clung to the outer shell of her calm for the old man's sake. She had a feeling of desperation. His voice kept on but she heard no more that he was saying. "Grandfather," she broke in at last.

"Sarah?"

"Before Mrs. Monteeth comes back . . . There is something . . . You have often said I should go back to Japan."

"I have said so, Sarah. I do sometimes think you got your ghosts there and there you must shake them off."

"Some day, Grandfather," she said strongly, "you'll find that I've gone. I won't be here. I want you to know and understand and not worry."

"Will you run away, Sarah?" She nodded. "With David?" he asked her.

"No, no, no. When I run away it'll be where he can't find me."

"I am glad you told me," he said solemnly. "I will understand. But it can't be soon, Sarah." He touched the bandage on her arm.

"Yes, it can," Sarah said resolutely. "Just as

soon as I can possibly drive my car with these arms.''

Grandfather pursed his lips. Mrs. Monteeth came bustling in.

"You know I must." Sarah's voice was sad. "The risk is too much. . . . If any more trouble came to him I couldn't live. . . ."

"Perhaps it is the wisest thing," the old man answered. "Poor Sarah, I know you are not happy."

Mrs. Monteeth rattled a glass sipper into the drink of cider and held it for her to sip. "*I* can hold it," Sarah said fiercely and she made her fingers pull around the glass to test the quality of the pain in her wrist that the moving muscles cost her.

"Now, rest," said Grandfather, "and I, too must be alone and rest. The arms must soon heal, eh? Mrs. Monteeth will watch over you," he beamed, "and let no one near."

"Thank you for everything, Grandfather," said Sarah and held her eyes tearless until he was gone.


Grandfather trotted down the corridor past his own and Malvina's bedroom doors. He peered into the big room and began to cross its emptiness. He saw Malvina and Edgar together out on the sea terrace beyond the dining room, a space from behind whose glass wind shelter the whole cove lay sparkling under the eye.

They were not looking at the view. Malvina was speaking earnestly and Edgar was absorbed.

Grandfather peered into the garden. Gust Monteeth was out there trying to repair the damage to the plants at the garage end. Grandfather took some keys from the table drawer where the household kept the car keys. He crossed the garden. He peered past the broken fence. No red car was there.

"Gust, can you go to San Diego for me?" said Grandfather briskly.

"Yes, sir." Gust straightened his back.

"I want you to run down tonight and be on the dock in the morning."

"Fresh fish, eh?" Gust grinned. He was used to Fox and these sudden orders. If you gave in and did what the old man said, the old man was not a bad employer. It was a good job, nice place.

"Yes. Now go to Andy's and he'll pack it for you. He knows just what I like. And get along right away, Gust. It's a long drive. It's getting late."

"What car can I use, sir? The Cadillac ain't—"

"Take Dr. Perrott's," said Grandfather. "Here are his keys. I'd rather he didn't leave the house anyhow while Miss Sarah may need him."

"I could take Miss Sarah's Chev—"

"Now, Gust, do as I say," said Grandfather petulantly.

"Yes, sir."

When Gust, in fifteen minutes, had changed to a clean shirt and trousers and gone off, nodding to Grandfather's last instructions, the old man stood on the lower level, the parking apron. No one could see him, here in this pocket. Two cars nudged the hill. Grandfather walked toward one of them. He pushed the glove compartment button. Oh yes, very happily, Sarah's driving gloves were here and Grandfather's clever hands were, of course, very small.

106

# Chapter 9

David paced Consuelo's floor. "It's all very well to say find out. Find out if the fire was set and who set it. Get evidence, you say. But there are experts to do that, Consuelo, and they're not getting anywhere."

"Just so you calm down, Davey." Consuelo twisted her beads.

"I'm pretty near too upset to think straight myself," he confessed. "But that silly girl . . ."

"Unfortunate haunted frightened girl," said the old lady. "You shouldn't expect too much of her, Davey."

"I *know* that."

"She's been alone. Now, I presume, she's in love with you, which makes it worse."

David stopped walking.

"Don't pretend to be astounded, either," said Consuelo. "You've guessed she is. So have I. Or why would she lash herself over *your* troubles?"

"Oh, Lord," he said and sat down.

"I'm glad you've lit," said Consuelo. "This summer matting isn't built for the wear and tear you're giving it. Now, while you are pulling yourself together, let me tell you about my telephone call. I talked to London. I remembered who would know what happened to Malvina's parents, so now I can tell you. Her father shot her mother and then himself when she was fourteen years old."

David whistled.

"Yes, it turned Malvina very cynical. She threw herself away, after that. She didn't care much for the rules anymore. I suppose it spoiled her. Bent the twig."

David said, "She's an odd girl, Consuelo. Strange mixture. Very calm and bland and very devious, I think. She likes intrigue. She's twisty."

"Twisted," sighed Consuelo charitably. "Well, I still don't like her but I suppose I ought to feel sorry for her."

"There's a limit to feeling sorry. If she's in the business of twisting *Sarah* I'll put off being sorry for Malvina."

"Davey, are they all in it?"

"For all I can tell. Who knows?"

"Snakes," said Consuelo. "A whole nest of them. Better think, Davey. Pin something down."

David batted his crown with his palm. "Now, was the fire set? That's the first thing. I'd say it was. Too much to believe in an accidental fire on top of all the rest. Who set it, then? I didn't and when I left the studio, nothing was burning. Malvina didn't set it. She went with me. Edgar didn't set any fire unless he used a mighty long fuse. He left, Mrs. Monteeth says, about as soon as I did. And he didn't go into the studio at all. That leaves Fox. Fox went in there. But Mrs. Monteeth was in there after him and she saw nothing burning. And if *she* set the fire, I'll be dumbfounded. The old soul is an automaton.''

"Somebody could have wound her up?"

David shook his head. "She'd say so. She's too mechanical to conspire. Gust wasn't near the place, or the Chinaman, either.''

"So it leaves Fox? Her own grandfather!"

"Any of them could have used a long fuse. And of course, it also leaves Sarah.''

"Sarah herself? Surely that's ridiculous!"

"*I* think so. But the arson expert was wondering. Her lighter was all the evidence they found. Edgar pretends to think she may have groggily dropped an open lighter and won't remember. But listen, Consuelo. I feel there is going to appear, sooner or later, a slight current of suspicion that Sarah might have done it on purpose.''

"Why?" gasped Consuelo. "Why ever would she?"

"Edgar will give out with some of his psychological hints," said David gloomily. "Sarah did it to keep the series going. To burn my stuff. She didn't intend to hurt herself. Well, it's true. You'd think, with her head cool, she could easily have gotten out of there.''

"What was she doing when you got in?"

"Try to *save* my stuff," said David, "or so it seemed to me.''

"It won't work, Davey. She wouldn't have wanted to burn your stuff.'' David seemed to groan. "*Why* would she want to keep this series going?" Consuelo demanded.

"Why?" he said. "If she's been fixing or lying about *all* these accidents. All by herself.''

"That would mean," said Consuelo in a moment, "that she is what we used to call crazy.''

"So it would." David turned up the toes of his

109

shoes and stared at them. "Mind you, Edgar doesn't say that. Malvina doesn't say that. But it's in the air. They pretend to be bravely ignoring the possibility. Malvina's very good at ignoring something so bravely that you can't help seeing what she means."

"I'm worried," said Consuelo.

"So am I. Especially since Sarah says she was asleep when the fire started."

"Don't you believe her?"

"I don't understand it. Fox says she was asleep. Mrs. Monteeth says she was asleep."

"Maybe she was asleep," said Consuelo brightly.

David said, "When I left her she was in a panic. Fifteen or twenty minutes later, she was sound asleep. Edgar says she took a headache pill but . . ."

"Where did she get it, Davey?"

"Huh? I wonder! David struck his thigh. "Now, by gum, I wonder!"

"Didn't you ask her? Isn't there any thought she may have been drugged? Wouldn't the doctor know?"

"Maybe he wouldn't tell. Yeah," David drawled. "Ye—ah. Listen, I didn't ask her much . . . because I couldn't get her to the point of hearing me until it was too late. Tried to tell her my new book is safe but I don't think she even got *that*. She was in such a . . ."

"Oh, Davey," said Consuelo sadly and reproachfully.

"I know. I know. Got to talk to her some more. Couldn't make a fuss and have the old man collapse. They . . . *he* ran me out of there."

Consuelo gnawed a knuckle. "Would you know if she wasn't quite right, Davey? I don't know the

110

girl, God help her."

"She sure was unreasonable this morning. I felt like socking her for a minute."

"Oh come, now," said Consuelo, cheering up. "After all, being in love with you doesn't necessarily mean she's off her rocker."

His eyes fled away from hers. "I tried . . . I wish now . . ."

"Yes, you should have," said Consuelo calmly.

He looked up, startled.

"Smacked her a good one," Consuelo said.

"A good *what*, Consuelo darlin'?"

"Ah, Davey, you know I mean a good sound kiss."

"I near as almost did," he confessed sheepishly. He had a sharp image of Sarah's beautiful mouth. "You're right. I wish I had." He was up, pacing again. "I wish she didn't trust the old Fox the way she does. She does, you know. Of course, it may be he's not in it. I wish she hadn't been in such a state."

"Didn't help her ·much," said Consuelo severely, "that stuff about proposing marriage."

"Edgar assumed it. I let it go. I had to get rid of him."

"Davey, you've got to get straightened around with that girl."

"Don't I know it!"

"Wait. Say. It *did* get rid of Edgar?"

"What do you mean?"

"Why? Why did he let you send him away?"

"Well, possibly Edgar wouldn't mind if I took up with Sarah. He may fear Malvina might take a shine to me."

"Now wait a minute, Davey. You say they made it difficult for you to talk to Sarah alone?"

111

"They sure did. Even this morning, Fox comes a-trotting, heart condition and all. You can't tell me he didn't deliberately interrupt."

"But *Edgar* would just as soon you *married* Sarah?"

"Well . . ."

"Well, they aren't seeing eye to eye then," cried Consuelo. "So, roil 'em up!" She made a rotary motion of her wrist that set her diamonds flashing. "Put them against each other."

*"That's* a female-type idea!"

"Davey, you haven't the least idea *why* all this is happening to Sarah?"

"No."

"And you are afraid they may all be in it?"

"Yes. I think it's possible."

"Then roil 'em up," said Consuelo firmly. "And don't hang around here talking to me. I kinda wish you hadn't left her up there."

"What could I do?" demanded David. "If I raise an open row, they tell me the old man will drop dead. I can't be responsible for that. What can I prove, anyhow? How could I get her out of there when she won't have anything to do with me?" He paced.

"Davey, do you want to marry Sarah Shepherd?"

"I don't think so," he said evenly. "I hadn't thought about marriage, you know. I was looking for a secretary."

Consuelo shook her dyed locks. "Maybe it's none of your business."

"None of my business!" He stopped still.

"You could give up."

"Give up!" he yelped. "Listen, whatever I think about Sarah, how can I let her go mad or get killed? And she could get killed. They used my car to kill one woman already. And they've burned up my work or so they think, and they don't care. None of my business!"

Consuelo said, "I'm thinking of your mama, Davey. I don't know how safe it is for you to go tangling any more with those people."

"If I thought it was safe," said David furiously, "I wouldn't have to do it. And it sure as hell isn't safe up there for Sarah, poor little owl."

"Owl?" said Consuelo.

"She . . . well, she wears glasses. She's got this cute little nose. She's blonde. I'm damned sorry for her. She's not to blame for being in a state. Most people couldn't take half as much. She's *intelligent,* Consuelo."

"She is, eh?" Consuelo folded her mouth and looked wise. "Well, then," she said in a moment, looking as grim and fierce as she could, "my advice is this. Go back. Watch out. Roil them up. Kiss that intelligent Sarah as soon as possible and bring her to me."

"My sainted aunt," said David, cocking a startled eye at her. "You may be right. I think I will do as you advise."

# Chapter 10

By the time David put Consuelo's car beside the other two that nudged the hill like suckling pigs, the afternoon was waning. He went up the blackened steps into the garden.

The ruined end of the building, the bent and broken fence, the odor of ugliness and destruction, hung over the garden and spoiled its peace, unless you faced the west and held your breath. Malvina was there, facing east and all the ugliness. Waiting for him.

When he saw her his heart stopped and he thought, *No, Lord, not my little owl. Nothing bad to her!* He knew that guilt and blame and self-reproach were hanging, ready to fall upon him for having left her even a few hours. So he understood Sarah better, even while he walked warily toward whatever it would be about her.

Malvina was dressed for dinner already in a frock of red linen, cut square and low, with wide straps crossing the tan of her plump shoulders. She had a stole of white wool on her arm and now she swung it around her. "David . . ." Her face was grave.

"What is it?" he demanded sharply.

"I don't like telling you this . . ."

"Go on." He didn't believe she didn't like it.

"You can't come in," she said. "Sarah thinks you have gone away."

"Who told her I had gone away?" he said. His blood seemed to start through his veins again.

"We did. We had to. There was nothing else to do to make her calm. Since we told her, she is better. So you can't come in. I'm sorry."

He said, "I don't believe you."

"David. David." She ran after him. "Grandfather is in the big room. It's cocktail time. Don't, don't . . . You know what we fear. Any excitement at all might . . ."

"I don't want any excitement. I want to be sure."

"Sure of what, David? Sarah does think you have gone. I told her so myself."

"Whose idea was this?"

"We had to. She doesn't want you here. You made her cry this morning. She told you to go. She begged you to go."

But David remembered Sarah's mouth nerving itself to say "So long."

"I don't understand," he said coolly. "You'll have to excuse me for wanting to understand it. Did your grandfather think of this idea?"

"No, no. We can't upset Grandfather either."

"Isn't this his house?"

David walked toward the glass door. Malvina caught at him. He could see she was angry because he would not move in the pattern she had designed. "Are you so wild about Sarah that you can't take no for an answer?" she cried. "Don't you care for an old man's life?"

"I care for most lives," said David quietly. "I

116

even care for the lives of innocent people walking in public places."

Malvina was breathing deeply. She was close. He could smell her perfume as if it were rising from her skin in a sudden cloud. She said nothing.

"However," said David calmly, "I think it only courteous to keep a promise."

"What promise?"

"I promised Sarah not to leave her. If I must leave her I should at least say goodbye."

"You are not a courteous man," she said angrily. "You are stubborn. You are intrusive."

"I was well brought up, just the same," said David imperturbably. And he opened the door and stood aside gallantly for a lady to enter. Malvina gave him one helpless angry roll of her eyes and stepped in.

It seemed to David that the old man was furious. Although he did not raise his voice beyond the slight whine that David had heard in it before, and the duckings and tiltings of his head were only a little more rapid, still there was strain in the neck chords and a bursting look about the eyeballs.

"Discourtesy," Grandfather was saying mournfully. "That a guest of mine should be told to leave. No, no, dear boy. You will stay on, if only to show me that you appreciate it was not discourtesy. It was only Malvina's mistaken attempt to confort our Sarah. Mistaken, of course. And I shall be mortified if you do not stay. Mortified. Now please do not go on talking of leaving."

David hadn't been talking. Fox was doing the talking. David had simply walked in and laid the whole situation quietly on the line. "Malvina tells

117

me I must leave. Because Sarah has been told I've gone." He'd made a bald quiet statement and sent the old man into this concealed rage.

Now David made one more statement, as quietly as before. "Since I promised Sarah I would not leave, may I make sure she knows?"

"Of course Sarah must know," said Grandfather irritably. "Malvina has been stupid. Oh, these well-meant lies! It's not as if you had to bother Sarah. You must stay as *my* guest, and Sarah must know it. My dear David."

"Grandfather," said Malvina in a voice curiously flat, "I acted for the best. Believe me, you mustn't . . ."

The old man put his hand on his chest, but his glance was lightning. "Now, Malvina, I am calm. I am very calm. But I cannot speak of this much longer. Edgar, take David along. Look in on poor Sarah. Quickly. Come back, then, and let us have our quiet chat before the fire. Since David is kind enough and courteous enough himself not to leave my house and mortify me."

"I will do nothing at all to upset you, sir," said David.

Edgar got up. "I'm not sure, sir . . ."

"You must all do as I say," snapped Grandfather.

They walked down the corridor, David last. "I can't leave now," said David softly. "We must think of his health."

Edgar stopped at Sarah's door and turned his head. His face was grim. His little eyes reddened around the rims. "You're not as smart as you think you are," he growled.

"Then tell me . . ."

But Edgar jerked his shoulders and tapped on

the door, opened it, and they stepped within.

She was alone, lying against the pillows, looking completely lax and spent as if there was no starch in her at all. David felt his anger rising. There she lay, paralyzed by all this nonsense. A pretty, intelligent young woman who ought to be living and working and looking around her, imprisoned in this room instead by a superstitious idea and the apathy of despair.

He said briskly, "Hello, Sarah." Her eyelids scarcely moved. "For the love of Mike, where are your glasses!" he said. "You look *terrible* without them."

Her eyes flew open in astonishment. Her hand went fumbling for her glasses on the table.

"I came to announce that the rumor of my leaving was a false one. Seems Malvina thought it was a good idea to lie to you."

Sarah didn't speak.

"Malvina was acting for the best," said Edgar stiffly. "You've misunderstood her."

Sarah's lips parted but she didn't speak.

"Malvina says it was the only way to get you calm," David prodded.

"That's not so," said Sarah feebly. But a little life came into her face.

"Well? Don't you care?" David challenged, fanning that spark. "Don't you *mind* that people tell you lies and lie about you? Are you going to shake and shudder in that bed and let people tell you whatever they please, true or false? Didn't you hear me say I wouldn't leave you? Did you think I had broken my word so soon? Didn't it cross your mind that *one* of us had deceived you?"

Her mouth was tightening. He thought he must . . . must . . . at whatever cost, keep on breaking that terrible apathy. "I've deceived you plenty," he said boldly. "Look at that piece of paper you rescued, why don't you?"

"What? Wait a minute." Edgar snatched the scorched fragment from where it lay. "I can't read it," he complained.

"Sarah can." David grabbed it and gave it to her. She looked at it. David met her widening eyes. "Now do you see how you suffer for *nothing?*"

"What do you mean?" Edgar was nervous.

"She knows."

Color was coming into Sarah's cheeks. The woeful, the wan, the forlorn look was vanishing. "I see how you deceived me," she said primly. She raised up. David saw with pleasure that she was getting angry. "Mr. Wakeley, did your car roll down a hill?"

Now he staggered. "Yes," he admitted.

"You didn't tell me so?"

"No."

"That was a kind of lie, I think," said Sarah.

"I beg your pardon," David said gently, "for all these things. But you suffer—therefore people spare you. You are *asking* for lies when you act as if you are not tough enough for the truth."

"Did you intend to ask me to marry you this morning?" she inquired. She was supported on one elbow; her head was tipped over. She looked at him steadily. She was good and mad.

"No," he said. "Not really."

"Then you lied to Edgar. Did anyone ask you to lie in that way?"

"No." David stood foursquare, intent upon her. "But I *have* lied. Don't you wonder why?"

He felt Edgar's hand trying to turn him and he snapped, "Doctor, is she so ill she must lie there?

Why can't she get up and fight like a human being?"

"You don't understand," said Dr. Perrott intensely. "Believe me, you don't know what it's all about. Now, come out of here. Now please, come away."

David was perceptive enough to feel the man's sincerity. He was willing to concede that there were things he did not understand. The man's urgency now made him doubtful. "All right. As long as Sarah knows I did not leave. I hope you are better, Sarah." He felt sure she was. She was good and mad, and he was glad of it.

She sat bolt upright and the soft fabric of her gown fell low on her bare shoulders. "You were very kind to come and tell me," said Sarah.

He could have sworn that proudly, toughly, she meant it. He couldn't answer. He let Edgar draw him away.

In the corridor Edgar said, "You do her no favor to teach her to think people lie, you know."

"No?"

"Symptom," snapped Edgar.

"Paranoia . . ." David's step faltered.

"You think of that a little late. Let her *alone*."


Sarah lay back and stared at the wall. Then she rolled and retrieved the charred sheet of David's notes from the floor. *Clinton*, she read. Then a line lower, *Howe*. Both British generals in the War of the American Revolution. They had nothing to do with the history of the State of California. These notes were old, made for David Wakeley's earlier book, already published. These notes had no value. It didn't matter if they burned. He hadn't even brought his real work here. He had not lost it. Nothing evil had happened to him.

Because he had deceived her. He had not meant to work with her at all. But why? She thought, So, I've been *spared*, have I? Of all the ridiculous . . . ! What is going on? she cried to herself. And something loosened and her heart swelled and she was good and mad and head-over-heels in love.

"Listen to me, Grandfather," Malvina said, as soon as they were left before the fire. She leaned across the cushions. "There is something you don't know. If you had let me in, this afternoon . . . but you wouldn't. You wouldn't listen. That car David is driving doesn't belong to him. It belongs to Consuelo McGhee."

Fox's jaws opened and and closed several times as if he ate and digested this.

"So we *must* get him away." She was triumphant. "Now you see, don't you? Now tell him you have changed your mind and make him go."

"Malvina, Malvina," said the old man, leaning back. The firelight played on his craggy face. "Never do that again. You must always do as I say." But the fire had gone out of his scolding for the moment.

"He is dangerous. Mrs. McGhee is dangerous. You've always said so."

"I will tell you because I see you must understand my plans. You are not to tell this to Edgar. Now . . ." He leaned forward and brought up his hands and began to smack the right fist into the left palm. "Sarah is frantic, afraid for David." Smack, went his hand. "If David stays, Sarah will run away." Flesh thudded on flesh. "Sarah will

122

run away as soon as her arms permit her to drive her car." Smack, he struck his palm. "Her car will take her over the brink at the first turn when she brakes to go around it." The hands came thudding together. "Because I have arranged that it should." Smack. "Now, do you see?"

Malvina looked stunned.

"It's not safe, Grandfather. What if Gust or Moon should take Sarah's car?"

"No one will take Sarah's car but Sarah. Because you will hold her keys. You will not put them with the others or in Sarah's room, either. When Sarah wants to know where they are, then you will give them to her. And not before."

Malvina took the keys that he gave her. She put them into a deep slit pocket at the end of her woolen stole.

"Yes?" he demanded.

"Yes, Grandfather." Her face looked baffled. All her instincts for intrigue, for the manipulations of people and events, came from this man. But he was her master. She could not outdo him in it.

"It's so simple," Fox said, relaxing. "So easy and clever, eh? She will sneak away, you see. Perhaps by night. Perhaps some morning when we are not noticing. We will be quite genuinely surprised." Then he looked angrily at her with his sharp little dark eyes. "But if David Wakeley leaves here, as you so foolishly tried to persuade him to do, then Sarah will not run away."

'But Grandfather, won't he . . . how can we keep them apart? What . . . ?"

"You can keep him occupied," snarled Fox. "Attach him, Malvina. Don't you think you can? Surely you are more of a woman then pallid little Sarah?"

Her face was both shrewd and stupid. "Edgar won't like it."

"Edgar. Edgar is a fool. Tell Edgar it is policy. Do as I say. Sarah's injuries won't hold her long."

"How long?"

"A day. Two days. Three at the most. Nothing to do but wait, Malvina. I have arranged everything."

"Grandfather . . ." Malvina bit her lip. "The first time Sarah drives her car, whether David is here or not . . ."

His jaws chewed on it. "And when will that be?" he said finally. "When will she? Eh? Sarah has nowhere else in the world to go, has she, Malvina? And no reason to leave me and go there. Are you willing to wait weeks, months, when we can, by keeping David here, drive her away in days?" His eyes were perfectly cruel. "Will you do as I say?"

Malvina said, "Attach him?" She was a little numb about many things—scruples, for one thing. Death, for another. If she had any attachment it was to this old man of her blood. One more thing. She had never known a man like David Wakeley. He had made her angry and she had shown it. He was a challenge. Malvina drew on veils and masks. Her mouth formed its frank and generous-appearing smile.

David and Edgar were returning. Malvina turned her head.

"I've been scolded," she said humbly, lids hinting at fires beneath the humble mask. "Will you forgive me, David?"

"I don't think we'll talk about it," said David as easily as he could, "since Mr. Fox has cleared up the whole thing."

"Grandfather is so clever," Malvina said.

＊　　＊　　＊

Sarah's light was out. She was not asleep but lying quietly abed when someone tapped lightly on her door. She crept to open it.

"Not asleep so early, dearie?" said Grandfather. "I thought I'd say goodnight."

"Is it early, Grandfather?" In the light that came across the corridor from Grandfather's door, Sarah's face was naked without her glasses.

"Perhaps not. Perhaps not. David and Malvina are still on the sea terrace, so I assumed . . . Are you feeling better, poor Sarah? Do your arms pain?"

"Not too much," she said.

"Goodnight." He peered at her face and nodded as if he were satisfied.

"Goodnight, Grandfather."

She closed the door but she did not go back to bed. She stood still for a minute or two and then she fumbled for her quilted coat and threw it around her shoulders. She felt for her glasses on the bedside table and put them on.

She intended to know what was going on.

She left her room and walked, barefooted, down the corridor. Into the big room where only one lamp burned. The dining room was all shadow. She saw the silhouette against the night light of the sky that lay beyond the great dining-room window. A dark shape, huge shoulders bent, and on them a small head.

Edgar was on his knees in the dining room, leaning beside the glass. Sarah drew nearer and he turned his head. He rose to his feet without a word when he saw her. He walked away toward the small square foyer. She saw him against the dark glass of the garden door, dimly, and then, silently,

125

he vanished. The whole movement was tragic, ominous.

Sarah drew nearer the window.

They were out there, Malvina and David, talking. She could hear the rhythm of their voices and it was gay. Malvina sat, wrapped in her white wool, on the sea terrace beside him, and together they overlooked that stunning view of sea and cove and sky. Together they enjoyed the starlight and the sea sound. They were very companionable and easy, she thought. They were alive.

As she watched, David lit a match and she saw his face and his smile. Malvina took his wrist in her fingers to steady the flame. Sarah turned and walked back across the living room.

She went into her room and closed the door. She sat upon the bed.

David had deceived her and was here not to work but for reasons of his own. And Malvina had lied. Malvina had definitely lied, black for white. Now the word David had used in the morning came back to her. An enemy.

She heard Malvina say, again, "How are you, Sarah? David has gone. I suppose you know."

"I didn't." Sarah felt again the surprise, part relief, part sorrow.

"Well, he's cleared out, bag and baggage. And who can blame him? So we are just the family," Malvina had said.

Nothing to misunderstand. Nothing to be charitable about. It was a flat lie. Because he had not gone. Now Malvina sat on the sea terrace with David Wakeley in the beauty of this night. Oh, she did, did she?

Sarah felt her face burning. She heard David saying, "Believe there is a reason . . . No such

126

thing as a Jonah . . . I'm talking about an enemy."

She said to herself, What if I have an enemy, after all? If I do, why, it must be *Malvina*.

Sarah knew she was angry and jealous. She rejoiced in it. Maybe it was small and childish, but it was good. It was human. It was living. David had deceived her and she was angry with him (although she believed he'd had a reason). But if Malvina was her enemy, then she could fight. And with relish, too.

"I will get up tomorrow and go about my business," she said out loud. She put her feet under the covers. There is a reason, she said to herself, for everything that has happened. I must find out. I must talk to Grandfather about money. I must talk to lots of people, to the police, to firemen, to the bank that foreclosed that time . . . to anyone who might know about any of these accidents. I'll manage for myself. I won't wait, either. Wrists are not too bad. I will begin. I will drive to the city tomorrow and I will begin to fight.

She snuggled down. No, she had never liked Malvina. She thought it was most probably the Lupino blood.

As for David Wakeley, not once yet, in his presence, had she let herself be Sarah. But if there was no Jonah, then there was more than one way to fight. Sarah smiled in the dark. Nothing—not anger, not insult, not Malvina on the terrace—had destroyed the unreasoning conviction that she and David drew closer and closer in a certain companionship. This strange sensation, this bubbling in the breast . . . ? Sarah remembered it. Happiness.

# Chapter 11

Before dawn, Sarah wakened. No, it was just dawn. First dawn. Sombeody was talking in a low but impassioned voice. And somebody else was trying to break into the stream of words. Who? Where?

Sarah slipped out of bed and went toward her door. Somebody was in the corridor. She put her ear to the wood.

Edgar.

"And no use and no use . . ." he said, "no use at all. You don't care for me, Malvina, and never will. Oh, you can hurt me with pity and you do hurt me, but I care too much for you, Malvina. I won't let you hurt yourself, Malvina."

"Please. Not here. Please." That was Malvina.

"Sorry for me. You tell him you're sorry for me. Just as he tells you he's sorry for Sarah. Sorry, Malvina? When somebody cares too much? Oh yes, the two of you are sorry. Have pity."

"Hush. Be quiet."

But Edgar's voice went on, so charged with emotion that it was almost a singsong, a wailing, a keening. "I told you there was a line and now I tell you that you won't cross it. . . ."

"Quiet!"

"No, I will not be quiet. Anymore. Anymore. Anymore."

"Then come out of the house. You'll be heard."

"Oh yes, I'll be heard. But you won't do anymore, Malvina. For your own sake, Malvina, I won't let you do anymore."

"Hush, hush, hush."

"No more . . . enough. No more . . ."

Sarah could tell that they were moving away. She raced for her quilted coat and her glasses and her Chinese slippers. This was a chance to find out something!


David Wakeley had heard Edgar leave the guest house. All night long, wakening intermittently, he had been aware of Edgar's suffering. He'd almost wanted to knock on the wall and say to the man, "Look, it's nothing. There is a game being played. And that's all. Don't take it so seriously." But then he remembered Consuelo saying "Roil 'em up," and he had beaten down his conscience and lain low.

All evening, responding to Malvina's beckoning mood, discounting all her hints and airs, David had been digging for information. He had turned up little or nothing. What? That Malvina had come to America in 1946. A fact he had known already. That it had been her first visit. A fact? That she had not known Sarah well until Sarah came here. They had met briefly as children, Malvina said.

What did it add up to? Not much. Ergo, Sarah had once been in England. Surely a meager

130

enough deduction.

He couldn't fathom Malvina. Why she had blazed at him in the garden and flirted at the dinner table he did not know. It was a game of cheat and maneuver. A game, yes. But he wished he hadn't started any game with Sarah Shepherd.

Just at dawn, he heard Edgar moving violently around his room. Then Edgar went out.

So David dressed.

He was at the window of his pleasant room in the small cottage, watching between the blinds, when Malvina in heavy black pajamas with her white stole thrown around her as if she'd had no time to reach for another garment, and Edgar, fully dressed for day, came out into the garden. They were arguing as they went along toward the place where the gate had been. David wished he could hear. He opened his door. Then he saw Sarah.

She was wearing yellow pajamas under a short pale green quilted coat and she came quickly out of the house and then hesitated near the fountain looking . . . owlishly, he thought fondly . . . about her. David forgot Malvina. He hurried across the garden.

"Sarah, let me talk to you."

"Yes, I want to talk to you." She faced him. This was not an apathetic figure, this taut little body, this face turned up coolly, the eyes steady. "What did you mean about money?" she asked briskly. "Do you think I have an enemy who doesn't want me to inherit?"

"Well, I wondered," he said, taken aback by her brisk manner. "I don't mean I'm sure of it."

"Because I am to get part of Grandfather's money?"

131

"Yes, I suppose so."

"Do you think she is trying to kill me?" said Sarah in fact-finding accents.

"You mean Malvina?" He was staggered by the change in her.

"It must be Malvina," Sarah said, "if the money is involved. Grandfather has no other heir."

"I . . . I don't know, Sarah." He was the one who fumbled and stammered. "I doubt if it's altogether Malvina . . . Who told you about my car, Sarah?"

"Your car rolled downhill by itself? A woman died? Is that true?"

"Yes. Yes, that's true."

"Grandfather told me the truth," she said.

Again he was staggered. "It wasn't an accident. Somebody deliberately made my car roll. Tell me this, Sarah. Who was *not here* a week ago last Saturday?"

"*I* wasn't here," said Sarah. "So I can't tell you that. But you don't think my enemy is Malvina?"

"Wait a minute. There was another thing. What was it I wanted to ask . . . ?" David thumped his head. They were speaking so rapidly and somewhat at cross-purposes, the talk went too fast.

"You let Edgar think you were going to propose to me," said Sarah calmly, "to get rid of Edgar. That means you think Edgar is in it? He is my enemy, too?"

"Sarah, I'm sorry. I had to talk to you alone. I came here in the first place . . ."

"Not to do your work." She nodded.

"I came to find out who might have done that to my car. But, Sarah, please try to understand. I'm afraid for you, now."

"And sorry for me, too," said Sarah, smiling.

132

But now he had his balance and he pinned her gaze steadily. "Sarah, I'm not as 'sorry' as you think. I certainly don't care for the idea that somebody wants to hurt you. And I don't like to see you alone." He felt the need to hurry, to warn her, to tell her. "Sarah, don't trust these people."

She stepped away as if she knew that he wanted to grab her there in the morning light. "I don't," she said. "It all fits in with what they were saying."

"*What* were they saying?"

"What are they saying now?" She moved swiftly and he had to turn and follow her as she began to run through the garden toward the old gate.



Down by the broken gate, Malvina was pleading. "You can't. Edgar, you can't. It's taking revenge. But Grandfather *told* me to talk to David. I did *not* . . ."

"No use. I'm going. I've got to go."

"You can't go to the police. You'd be in such trouble . . ."

"Yes, I can go. I'm going to explain everything. Oh yes, my part, too. How I've lent myself to your grandfather's doings. Because I've been weak . . . weak. And you are not worth it, Malvina, but I love you and will love you . . ."

"Then, Edgar, think better of it. Don't do this now. We can talk. We can . . ."

"No," he said. "No, Malvina. No, I can't think better of it. Not any more."

"You'll go to a bar," she said lightly, her eyes glistening. "You'll think better of it. Oh, I'm sure."

"No. No bar open," he muttered.

"There is one place we know . . . Edgar, you

133

haven't slept well . . ."

"I can save you," he cried. "And I will, even though it's trouble. I must go." He started down the steps and stopped and turned his head dazedly. "Who took my car?"

"Gust has it. Grandfather sent him. . . . It's an omen. Edgar, don't go."

"Give me the keys to your car, Malvina."

"Oh no. It's not likely." She kept trying to be lighter, to play the coquette.

"Malvina," he said, fixing her with the tragic intensity in his little eyes. "For your soul's sake and before you do murder, let me save you. Let me go."

"You'll think better of it," she said, her smile frozen. "Dear Edgar . . ." Her fingers slipped into the pocket of her stole. "I cannot believe you will hurt me. See, I believe in you. Look, I have Sarah's keys. Take Sarah's car."

Sarah was opposite the tiny kitchen garden when she stopped. "Car. Edgar is leaving. Here she comes in again."

David, close behind her, said, "Sarah . . . Sarah . . ." He began to close his arms around her.

She gave a little scream of pain. "The burns . . . the burns!"

"Oh, Lord," he said, "I'm *sorry!*" and let her go. But for just one moment the meeting of their eyes was as close as a kiss.

Malvina was rising into the garden and she walked toward them on the brick-paved path, swaying, her head high, her smile in place. "Good morning," said Malvina.

As she faced them, smilingly, the sea's crashing

on the rocks continued and nearby birds cried. There was a cracking sound as of a limb breaking suddenly on a tree and it was lost in the natural hubbub. Neither David nor Sarah noticed it, nor the heavier sound, as of a monstrous breaker, that followed. Malvina's face was still innocently fresh and smiling when a thin scream from a human throat rose like a thread of smoke into the vault of the sky.

David turned around and looked over the garden wall. Someone on the beach far away in the cove was screaming and gesticulating. Then he saw the car, lying like a beached whale in the surf close below with foam boiling around it.

"Car! Look!"

"Where? Oh!"

"It's Edgar!" shrieked Malvina. "Edgar ran off the road!"

David's eye was calculating the swiftest way to descend. He said, "Phone the police, Sarah. They'll know who can help. Quick, Sarah." His eyes took time to send her courage and support.

"I will," she said. "All right, David."

Moon burst out of the kitchen, jabbering.

David was over the wall already. "Malvina, get a rope. Sarah, telephone." He was gone.

Sarah said, "Grandfather! Don't let him see!" She ran into the kitchen to the phone there.

Moon was at her shoulder, repeating one series of syllables over and over again.

Sarah made the call. She leaned on the kitchen counter to peer out and down. She could see people on the rocks now, some of them struggling in the water. She could see Malvina in her black pajamas kneeling on a rock. She couldn't go. Sarah could not help. Her arms were not healed enough. Sarah began to draw deep breaths.

"I must stay with Grandfather and be sure he is calm," she told herself out loud. "I must be perfectly calm myself, or Grandfather might die."

The Chinaman said that phrase again. "Yes, yes, I'll be careful," Sarah answered, and thrust out of her mind all that she could of wonder and of fear.

She moved quickly through the house toward Grandfather's room. Mrs. Monteeth was in the living room. Sarah warned her to make no sound. Told her quickly what had happened.

"Mr. Fox is having his early coffee."

"His bedroom? Good. I'll go keep him on the west side of the house. I'll be with him. Watch from the study, Mrs. Monteeth. And be quiet."

"Are you all right, Miss Sarah?"

"I've got to be."

She drew one more deep breath and tapped and when he answered, entered smiling.

# Chapter 12

Grandfather's bedroom was vast. The carpeting was crimson, thick and soft. The walls were gray. Across the western windows the draperies of crimson and gray had been half opened to the day. His huge bed had a fringed canopy of heavy white stuff and on his pillows the old man was enthroned. Music was playing softly.

"Ah, Sarah. Good morning. Are your arms better today, dearie?"

"Much better." She came near him and spoke lovingly. "Grandfather, are you feeling strong?"

He flicked his lids wider.

"There is a thing that has happened. It may not be too bad." She sat on the bed and took his small plump dry hand.

"Tell me, Sarah," Grandfather said, sinking upon his pillows. "I am strong."

So, as carefully as she could, she told him.

"Edgar's car?" he said frowning. "But Gust has Edgar's car in San Diego."

"It was gray," said Sarah. "Why, I suppose it was my car!" She beat down the jumping heart. She saw the cord of his neck, the bulge of his eye.

She stroked his hand. "It didn't drop so far. They will pull him out," she said soothingly. "Whatever happens, we cannot grieve for everyone, or so you said, Grandfather. Do you remember?" She watched him, dedicated to his welfare.

The old man drew his lips back from his teeth. "Where is Malvina?"

"Malvina has gone to help. And David, too. But I will stay with you, Grandfather."

"I must get up," he said petulantly. His eyes turned toward the door to his study.

"Better . . . not the study," Sarah said gently.

The old man plucked the blanket.

"Mrs. Monteeth is in the study, Grandfather, and from there she can see. People are doing all they can."

"I know. I know," he said restlessly.

"Moon will bring your full breakfast here. I will take a cup of coffee with you."

The old man's lids hid the eyes. "Thank you, Sarah," he said and over his face passed a wry look, almost as if . . . Sarah thought, wondering, watching him so carefully . . . almost as if something bitterly amused him.


The car had rolled and was now more or less upright. David threshed through the water. The door would not open but the glass had broken. He was holding the man's head high within the car when other hands came to help him pull Edgar out.

Mrs. Monteeth, from Grandfather's study, could see all these efforts. But Sarah remained within the quiet bedroom, holding herself from running to see, cut off from the news. Still, the old man was

138

calmer. The bulging look of the eye had receded.

Grandfather was even rather curious and prying as if he enjoyed the gossip. "They were quarreling?" asked Grandfather. "Whatever for?"

"I thought they were," said Sarah. "Edgar said he wouldn't be quiet. He wouldn't let her do any more."

"Do any more," said Grandfather slowly. "Is that all he said, Sarah?"

"All that I heard." She flushed. "There was something about love."

"Eh? Oh yes, love. Yes. Of course."

"Grandfather, there is something I've been meaning to ask you. It's about your will that you made."

"Why, Sarah? Why do you ask about the will? You and Malvina will have my money, of course. You don't mind, Sarah? You know that Malvina was good to me. We were so close in our sorrow when my dear old Lupino died."

"She is a Lupino," said Sarah under her breath.

"Eh? Sarah?"

"I don't know, Grandfather. I don't want to upset you, but I wonder . . ."

"Never fear," said Fox craftily. "Tell me, Sarah—" He seemed to snuggle toward gossip. His eyes were bright. "Has David asked about my will? Eh?"

"He . . . thinks I may have an enemy. Because of the money."

"Does he, indeed? My dear little Sarah. What nonsense, eh?"

"I just wonder," said Sarah. "It worries me, Grandfather. Because, you see, whoever it is may be your enemy, too." She gulped. "Oh, have I frightened you, shocked you?" She watched the narrowing of his eyes. "I am not being good for you."

"You are good for me, a good sweet child," he said. "And I am such an ancient man. Do you know, I wouldn't mind an enemy." He cocked his head and the tough and ancient dimples appeared on his hard cheeks. "Do you believe it?" he asked, twinkling as if this were a delight.

"Since Malvina lied to me, it makes me wonder . . ."

But he sighed. "Some people tell these stupid well-meant lies. Malvina is sometimes a little stupid, Sarah."

"Perhaps, Grandfather."

"But now you fear for me?"

She ducked her head, unable to speak.

"Well, then," said Grandfather softly, "you and I must never lie to one another. Dear Sarah, you must always tell me what you are thinking."

"Oh, I will," she promised. "I do."

But Sarah did not tell him. She did not cry out what she might have cried. In anger or in fear. Isn't it strange, isn't it odd, isn't it ghostly . . . that this has happened to *my car!*

About nine o'clock, Mrs. Monteeth tapped on the door. She entered the bedroom. "Gust has come back," she announced, nodding as if she knew good news. "He has picked up Miss Malvina. Miss Malvina is here."

"Send Miss Malvina to talk to me," said Grandfather at once. "Sarah, go dress. Do as I say, dearie. I am calm."

"Mrs. Monteeth, you stay." Sarah flew out the door to the corridor. Malvina was standing at her

140

bedroom door. Her black pajamas were soaked and plastered to her body. Her hair was wild, the knot loosened and falling out of its moorings. Her eyes looked stricken.

"Edgar is in the hospital," Malvina said hoarsely and wearily. "David got him out."

"Oh good! Oh good for David! Don't go to Grandfather like that."

Malvina's face tightened. "Do you think I don't know?" she said contemptuously and yanked her door open. Sarah followed her in.

"Malvina, what were you and Edgar quarreling about?"

"We were not quarreling."

"I heard you." Sarah thought, She is trying to lie.

"What did you hear?" Malvina had gone into her bathroom and the black pajamas fell on the floor soddenly.

"What was it he said you wouldn't do any more?"

Malvina came out of the bathroom with her yellow robe held around her. She was toweling her long black hair. "He was jealous, Sarah," Malvina said.

"I know. I know. Of you and David. But what was it he said he wouldn't let you do any more?"

Malvina's eyes flickered. "He said I wouldn't make him suffer any more." Malvina raised her head and shook it. She whacked her hair with a brush rapidly. Then, arms raised, she began to roll up the hair. "And I thought I had talked him out of it," she said bitterly.

"Out of what, Malvina?" Sarah leaned on the wall.

"Don't you know?" Malvina turned and her face

141

pitied Sarah's ignorance. "Didn't you realize? Edgar *ran* the car off the road."

"Oh . . . oh, you mean he wanted to . . . He tried to . . ."

"He was terribly upset."

Sarah was silent, tasting the credibility of the idea that Edgar had tried suicide.

Malvina said, "Don't worry. I won't tell Grandfather."

"Oh no! Oh no! You mustn't!"

"I'll tell him it was an accident," Malvina said, and then angrily. "Get out. I've got to dress. I must see Grandfather. Things to do. . . ."

"Yes," Sarah said. "Yes, all right, Malvina. But be careful."

Sarah went to her own room and dressed herself quickly. She put on a cotton shirt and a pair of brown corduroy slacks. She left her feet in the Chinese slippers. She was numb with all this news. A stray thought came to her. "Be careful." Why, she had understood Moon this morning. How was that? Now she knew he had been saying to her, over and over again, "Be careful." Perhaps, after having been in Japan, some of his syllables were familiar to her. Certainly she had understood that little bit. How strange. He had said to her "Be careful," and she had understood. Sarah's mind went to the news.

David, strong and quick, had saved Edgar's life. But Edgar had tried suicide. Sarah thought, No. Wait a minute. Edgar meant to be *heard*. He said he wouldn't be quiet. But to die is to be very quiet indeed. It's all *lies*, thought Sarah.

Fox said in his chirruping happy voice, "Then

our dear Edgar will be all right again? Ah, good news. Eh? Mrs. Monteeth, dear ma'am, quickly. Find flowers," he commanded. "Tell Gust he must take these girls to the hospital. Quickly. Ah yes. We must make a great fuss of Edgar. Poor chap. Poor fellow. Try to find roses," Grandfather cried.

Mrs. Monteeth went beaming and bustling.

To the angry old face on the pillow, when she had gone, Malvina spoke flatly. "Edgar was going to the police. To save my soul. So I did it. But David was too damned quick. Now Edgar is going to tell them everything." She looked beaten and sullen.

"Then hurry," Fox said. "To the hospital."

"He won't be quiet," she scoffed.

"He'll *see* you," Fox said. And he clambered out of the huge bed and threw his brocaded dressing gown around him. "In the study. Come. I told you. I have some poison."

"Grandfather . . ." She stumbled after him.

"You have been stupid, Malvina. And now you will have to manage."

"How . . . can I? They will know if I do."

"That's why Sarah is going too."

"Sarah?"

"Yes. Yes, and hurry."

They whispered furiously together.

"I can't do it, Grandfather."

"For me?" he said. "What is there to lose, Malvina?"

"Nothing, I suppose. Your life and mine." She shrugged and looked around her. "You'd better hide the rest of it. Be a search here."

"Yes," he said. "That is discerning of you, my dear. I will hide it well. Come now, I am not angry,

Malvina. I see that you acted quickly. I only want you to finish what you meant to do."

She shrugged again, but her mind had taken hold and went in the coils, the twists, the turnings of its habit.

"If you are bold," he said, "and quick. There now, Malvina. You are calm. You are clever, after all. You will manage."

The look of defeat was gone from her face. He seemed to have brought to life again whatever there was of Malvina.


Sarah found them in the living room.

"Come, Sarah," said Grandfather, in high spirits. "Take the flowers, dearie. Gust is going to drive you."

"Where am I going?" she gasped.

"To the hospital of course, dearie. To see poor Edgar."

"Yes," said Sarah loudly. "Yes, I do very much want to see Edgar."

"And she'd better get those arms dressed," said Malvina, "now that Edgar isn't here to do it."

"Now, she must," beamed Grandfather. "There. Give him my love, dears, and off with you. Quickly."

So it was no later than nine-thirty when Gust took them gingerly down the road in Malvina's car. Sarah saw people still on the rocks below. She couldn't spot David among them although she knew he was there. They were trying to figure out a way to raise the car.

She thought she must talk to David, to many people. But she asked no more questions of Malvina, who would only lie. They rode in silence, sitting apart.

At the small hospital a nurse said that Dr. Perrott could have no visitors, not just yet.

"Tell him my name," purred Malvina, her eyes glistening. "Tell him Malvina is here. Please. And can someone tend to Miss Shepherd's arms?"

"Of course," the nurse said. "If she'll come with me."

"Go on." Malvina gave Sarah a little shove. "We'll wait. We won't go until they let us see Edgar."

So Sarah found herself in a treatment room. The young doctor was encouraging. He said the arms were already healing nicely. "Had a lot of bad luck up at your place lately," he remarked cheerfully.

"Yes, it does seem so," Sarah said steadily.


Edgar was not even badly hurt, a rib or two broken, and the shock. He said without opening his eyes, "Malvina?" His voice was completely tragic.

She slipped into the room and crouched with her face close to his. "Grandfather," she said. "Edgar, take me away from him."

"I?" His eyes opened.

"So . . . dreadful. . . . He . . . blundering. . . . Trying to hurt Sarah. . . . Hurt you. . . . Edgar, marry me?"

The man's chest rose and fell rapidly.

"Here. Now," she whispered. "So I needn't go back. I never want to go back."

"Has to be time . . ." His head moved. He looked astonished and a little wild.

"Then let me get the licenses . . . whatever it is. Blood tests. And stay in the village. I have a little

145

money, Edgar. Enough. We can go away when you are better.''

"Malvina . . . Malvina . . ." He thrust her away so that he could see her.

"You were right. I see now. Now that this has happened. He is evil." Her lips showed her strong beautiful teeth.

"It's horrible, Malvina," burst Edgar. "Blundering . . . bumbling around with his hideous plots. Old and cruel and careless. Listening to nobody . . . He's like an evil baby playing with murder instead of a rattle.''

"Yes," she said. "Yes, he is."

"He'll come to his punishment. Oh, leave him, Malvina. Now that you know."

"I didn't know," she sobbed on his pillow. "I didn't know about the car. He told me to give Sarah those keys. It was for Sarah."

"Yes," he said with satisfaction. "Yes, it must have been for Sarah."

"Marry me. Save me." Her face touched his. Malvina could weep real tears. The moisture on his cheek convinced him. "You are not going to die," she wept. "We can go away together. Money doesn't matter."

"Mexico," he said.

"Anywhere . . ."

"Somehow," he said and now she knew she had convinced him by the purpose gathering in his body, by the rapidity of his heart.

"Don't say anything to Sarah," she whispered. "She is here. She's coming to see you. Tell David Wakeley," said Malvina. "Don't you see? *He* will get Sarah away from there."

"We . . . can't . . . leave Sarah . . . with the old man." Edgar looked dazed.

146

"No, no. But Sarah believes in him. And she will talk to him. And I'm afraid, Edgar. Until we are married. He can stop us, Edgar, if we are not careful. And he will not want me to get away. Oh, let us get away together. . . ."

"Get a message to Wakeley," said Edgar with sudden vigor. "Tell him to come here. Don't you go back to the Nest." His vigor failed and he added weakly, "Nor Sarah either."

"I'll send her to David. Let them do as they please. I won't go back. I will always be with you. If you had died, Edgar, *I* would have died."

"Malvina," he said and took her left hand and put it against his face and closed his eyes.

Therefore, Malvina's right hand was free to do what she had come to do.

"I hear somebody, darling," she said softly in a moment. "Oh, look at the flowers. How we have crushed them!"

"Malvina . . ."

"Do I look as if I've been crying?" She was smiling.

A nurse and Sarah came in. The nurse said, "Not much longer, please."

"How are you feeling, Edgar?" asked Sarah gently. She tried to read in his face whether he had meant to die. He looked excited, Sarah thought. Pleased and excited.

"Well enough . . ."

"He's fine," said Malvina with a catch in her voice. "Thank heavens. Nurse, may I use that vase?" She seemed tense and keyed up, too.

Sarah said, drawing closer to the bed, "We are so glad you got out of that. Grandfather sends his love."

"Does he?" said Edgar. "How are you, Sarah?"

He watched Malvina, who took the water pitcher and filled the vase and put the flowers in it.

The nurse, who remained at the door, said, "Only a minute more, I'm afraid. Dr. Perrott needs to be quiet."

"Oh yes, we'll be going," Malvina said brightly. "I've so much to do." Her eyes exchanged secrets with Edgar. "Sarah, move that glass, won't you, so I can put the flowers there."

Sarah took the water glass, which was two-thirds full, away from the small table beside the bed on which Malvina was setting the vase of flowers. She held it, wondering what to do with it, wondering what to say to Edgar.

"Pretty?" Malvina touched the flowers. "We must go, darling."

Sarah said, "But what happened, Edgar? The car went over, we know that. Please, was there anything wrong?"

The nurse rattled warningly. Edgar answered, looking only at Malvina, "There was something wrong. Sarah, you should get married."

"I should . . . what? Edgar, what do you mean?"

"It would be a good thing," Edgar said. "And safer." Now his face was tragic again. "Sometimes it is safer to marry. Isn't it, Malvina?"

"Edgar," Sarah cried, "you'll have to explain . . ."

He began to raise himself from the bed. His eyes never left Malvina. His breathing was heavier.

"Darling," Malvina said, "don't upset yourself. Don't worry. Everything will be all right. I will take care."

"I'm afraid you mustn't stay," the nurse said sharply.

"Can we do anything?" Malvina was solicitous.

"Are you thirsty? Isn't there something you would like?"

"Where is his glass?" the nurse said.

Sarah had the water glass. She put it on the edge of the table, in the lee of the flower vase.

"I'll get your pitcher filled," the nurse said. "Now, ladies, please . . ."

Edgar's eyes were fixed on Malvina. He looked very ill and tired now. He said, "Shall I wait for you, Malvina, a little while longer?" There was in his voice a great sadness and despair.

Sarah helplessly turned. He wasn't aware of her. She looked back. Malvina's hand was on his brow. Malvina said some soft word. Malvina kissed his brow and left his side. Sarah saw Edgar, tense and awkward, a look of hope and struggle on his face, reaching for the glass of water as the nurse bustled them out.

Gust was waiting. They got into the car. "Home, I suppose," said Malvina. Now, suddenly, she looked exhausted.

Sarah flexed her arms a trifle. The pain was not great. "Edgar says something was *wrong*," she said crisply. "What did he mean? What was wrong?"

"Of course something was wrong," Malvina muttered. "We had quarreled."

You said you hadn't, Sarah thought. But she skipped that and pressed another question. "You said you would *take care*, Malvina. Take care of what?"

"Of myself," said Malvina savagely.

Sarah remembered Edgar's words. *Safer to marry*. What did that have to do with Malvina taking care of herself?

"What about safety?" Sarah insisted. *"Who* isn't safe?"

Malvina looked at her angrily. "People around *you,*" she snapped. "You and your jinx. You and your Jonah."

"It's all lies," said Sarah quietly, and she sat quietly and was borne upward toward the Nest and Grandfather.

# Chapter 13

"Consuelo?" David in a phone booth was dirty and unshaven. His clothes had nearly dried upon his body.

"Davey?" Consuelo in her gaudy morning coat snuggled the phone closer. "Good morning."

"Not so good." His voice was grim. "Got a packet of horrors for you. Can you take it?"

Consuelo said, "Yep." She sat down, her fleshy body quaking. "Go on, Davey."

"Not Sarah. She's O.K. I just called the Nest. But listen, Consuelo. Sarah's car went off the road this morning with Edgar Perrot in it. He's O.K., or will be. I got to him before he drowned. Hospital now. He wasn't conscious. . . ."

"Wait a minute, Davey! *Sarah's car?*"

*"Exactly,"* he said. "Look, if you have any influence will you talk to this man Maxwell?"

"From the Sheriff's office?"

"Yes. I can't get anywhere. He doesn't know me. He thinks I'm a nervous swain or something. Nothing I say penetrates. We can't raise the car out of the water without heavy machinery. I doubt if there is going to be any evidence, anyhow."

"Wait a minute, Davey. Wait a minute. Evidence of what?"

"Of murder," said David. "Because that's what is going on. Call this Maxwell and do something. Vouch for me, at least. Will you, Consuelo? Meantime, I've got to run over to the hospital, see what I can get out of Edgar himself, and then . . ."

"Murder?" Consuelo said. "You mean murder for Sarah?"

"That's it. That's right."

"Davey, for heaven's sakes . . . !"

"I know. I know. Get her out of there. I will. I'm going to get her out of there, Consuelo. I don't care how, either."

*"Don't* you care," said Consuelo fiercely. "Hit her and drag her. Anything."

"I intend to. If I could just get one pennyworth of proof . . ."

"Oh, Davey, get her out of there first."

"I *know,*" he said.

"Bring her here."

David blessed her and hung up, thinking that it didn't cross Consuelo's mind to consider whether trouble went where Sarah came. He gathered himself and reviewed his plans. He did not like the shape of things. On the phone he had said to Gust Monteeth, "Stick as close as you can to Miss Shepherd. I'm afraid something might happen to her."

The man had taken this bald advice with very little surprise. "I know what you mean, Mr. Wakeley," he'd said, with a certain relish, a certain pleasure in an exchange of this kind. "Me and the Missus, we've heard Mr. Fox say he's afraid, many's the time. The little lady's had too much to take. Liable to feel pretty low in her mind. Yeah, we know that."

"Then watch her," David had snapped and hung up. But the old Fox had laid the ground for Sarah's suicide. Had he? Well, if Sarah had driven off the road and the car showed no incontrovertible evidence of any tampering, wouldn't the accumulation of Sarah's trouble add up to just this suspicion?

He hurried out of the drugstore across from the Sheriff's office and peered around for the taxicab he had ordered. He had no car, having hooked a ride with the Deputy and argued all the way. He'd talk to Edgar. He thought Edgar might tell him something. He thought even Edgar, stupefied and besotted as he was by his infatuation, could not deny that he and Malvina had been in dispute and immediately thereafter Malvina had, at the very least, *watched* him drive away in Sarah's car. If the car was a death trap, Edgar had not known it. But had Malvina known it? That was a good question to put to Dr. Perrott. It should have an interesting result, one way or another.

When the cab came he directed it to the hospital, and he had it wait for him, and that was a good thing because he was there four minutes. Long enough to hear how Edgar had died.

When the cab took him through the gates to the Colony Cove, David knew the Sheriff's car couldn't be far behind. He had in his hand a ring full of keys. Edgar's keys.

A rather stupid little clerk at the hospital had asked if any of Edgar's effects were needed by the family. He'd snatched the keys, signed something. It had been in his mind to search Edgar's possessions. Now he thought better of it.

He thought the confusion at the hospital would

soon clear. The Deputy Sheriff would not care for this idea. He shouldn't have been given the keys. He shouldn't have taken them. In the case of a natural death, this may have been normal procedure. The little clerk hadn't realized . . . Edgar had been poisoned. This was murder.

Open, he thought. *Good.* At least it's open. And someone will listen, now.

He paid the cab off and ran up the nine steps into the garden. He saw Gust puttering about a vine. "Where is she?"

"Miss Sarah? She's O.K.," Gust said. "She's with her grandpa."

David gave him a black look, and rushed across the garden. Malvina was standing in the small foyer, face frozen, phone tight to her ear. David strode into the big room. He saw through an open door the old man in his chair in the study, only a silhouette against the light. Before his heart stopped, Sarah came, with short quick steps, out of the study; she closed that door and came toward him.

He wanted to touch her and did not dare, remembering her pain when he had touched her before. As his hands came up she saw the keys he was holding.

"Edgar's?" said Sarah, and took them. "Oh, how is he now? We saw him an hour ago. He was pretty well. You saved him." Her face was glowing and admiring.

David thought only that he must save *her*. She must leave here alive. He didn't analyze the bare panic that now drove everything else from his mind. He said, "Sarah, will you go with me, now, quickly?"

"Go where?"

He thought of the Sheriff's car that wouldn't be far behind, whose arrival would freeze them all here, possibly. Was there time? How to shake her and shock her and get her away? He wished he dared touch her.

"Marry me," he blurted. "Sarah, throw the world over and come away with me, *now.*"

Her face wrung his heart. It was shocked and in the shock was joy. Deep in the eyes the confession lay open. But Sarah said quietly, "Why, David?"

He groaned. "Sarah, they are trying to kill you."

The eyes winced. "Malvina?"

"Yes, Malvina." (Anything, anything, to get her away.)

"But then I can't leave Grandfather," she stammered.

"Yes you can. Safer. Just let me take you where you will be safe. Sarah, run away with me." Her lips parted. She seemed to rise on her toes, to be falling toward him. "Gamble," he said, keping his arms from reaching for her lest he hurt her. "Do it. Jump off into the blue. . . ." While their eyes clung, he said gently, "We may be in love with each other." Her mouth trembled. He bent to kiss it. Consuelo was right. If only once his mouth were to touch Sarah's beautiful mouth, everything would be better, and he would know what truth to tell her.

But she swayed away and he saw by her eyes that Malvina was standing close behind him. He half turned. He knew at once what Malvina must have only just heard on the phone. It was impossible for him not to meet Malvina's eyes and confirm the news, even though he could have wished that this knowing glance did not have to pass between them in front of Sarah.

Malvina said with a grisly smile, "Did you see Edgar?"

David shook his head. "Too late."

Sarah said, "What are you talking about, please?"

But Malvina staggered, "Grandfather," she cried. "We must think of his poor old heart . . . and take care . . ."

Sarah caught her breath. David told her. "Edgar is dead."

David stood between them and it was Malvina who started to fall so it had to be Malvina he supported with a quick arm. "How can we tell him?" she mourned.

"I can tell him," Sarah said quietly.

"Eh?" said Grandfather. "Oh, there you are, David." He began to trot toward them. "Dear chap, aren't you going to catch a chill? Look at your clothing! Come now, what's the matter?"

Sarah gathered her control but Malvina was quicker. It was Malvina who said, "Grandfather, we have had some news. I'm afraid it isn't pleasant at all." Her voice was the old purr. Indeed, it was almost cheerful.

Sarah moved quietly near the little old man and put her hand on his arm. His fingers scrambled for hers and David Wakeley watched it. Watched her face, which was all tender anxiety, watched the old man, who was anxious, too. "I am ready," Grandfather said and the old lids guarded the eyes.

"Soon after we saw Edgar, he died, in the hospital."

"Ah . . ." The old man's head bent toward his chest. "Many have died. So many. Eh, Sarah?" Sarah had her arm under his, now, and he leaned upon her. "So many I have known. And I am an

156

old, old man and I do not die."

They helped him toward a chair.

"They are saying a very terrible thing," Malvina said. "Grandfather, I am afraid you must know. . . . They say Edgar has died of poison."

David watched Sarah's whole body take this shock. Her eyes came to his, stunned, unbelieving. He watched her, and not the old man. He watched her control any cry, any terror, and heard the old man say, "I don't wish to hear any more. Edgar is dead. That's what you say? Then, that is enough to hear in one morning."

"Of course it is. You must lie down, Grandfather."

"Yes, I . . ."

"Shall I call Mrs. Monteeth?"

"Yes, do, dearie."

"Yes, we had better," Malvina said. Both Monteeths came and the old man was led gently away.

David, waiting in the big room alone, moved to the sea side and looked out upon the scene. But he did not see it. He was seeing the lift of Sarah's head, the brace of her shoulders, the proud bone driven by the courageous heart. He knew that if he could he was going to marry Sarah Shepherd.

He also knew it was too late, now, to run away.

An official-looking car was threading swiftly through the houses in the cove.

# Chapter 14

They had taken chairs near the glass in the big room, Malvina, David, Sarah. The Sheriff's Deputy, Thomas Maxwell, who had come himself, had his own back to the light. The sense of being on an edge was here, as it was in so much of this house. Beyond the glass there seemed to be nothing, nothing at all but empty air.

"We see no reason to believe that the hospital staff is involved," he told them. His deep voice rumbled out of his chest and set up vibrations. "Dr. Perrott had no connection with the hospital. No one there knew him more than casually. But he had visitors. Miss Lupino, I believe you were one. And Miss Shepherd."

"Yes, we were both there," said Sarah tensely. Malvina said nothing. She smiled her false smile.

"Nurse tells me you two had been gone no more than twenty or twenty-five minutes when she discovered the death. Now we know that poison was put in his glass of water. Not the pitcher. The glass. We don't understand how he could have taken it in water and not known. Fact remains, he did. Now, the glass shows fingerprints. Did either of you handle it?"

"Yes. I did," said Sarah. "My fingerprints will be on it."

"Did you handle it, Miss Lupino?"

"No, sir."

"He had no other visitors," Maxwell said, "but you two young ladies."

"You are assuming that one of these two young women put poison in that glass?" said David, his hair seeming to stir.

"We have to check," the Deputy said smoothly. "Now, pending analysis, we have made a good guess as to what the poison was. An alkaloid. What drugs are in the possession of anyone in this house?"

"I don't know," said Sarah. Her face was cold with her fine control.

"Oh . . ." Malvina's eyes flickered as if with a sudden memory. "In Edgar's laboratory."

"Yes?"

"Down at the back of the garage." Malvina bit her lips and the eyes widened and turned in that hinting manner of hers. "I couldn't say what drugs he might have kept in there."

"Kept the place locked up, did he?"

"Yes," Sarah said. "I suppose you will want to look around in there. Here are his keys." She took Edgar's keys from the pocket of her slacks.

Malvina covered her face. Maxwell handed the bunch of keys to his companion, a man in plain clothes, without comment. The man made a salute indicating understanding and left the room. David sat still and kept quiet and an idea swelled rapidly and occupied his mind.

"Miss Lupino?" Maxwell prodded. "Something's come to your mind?"

Malvina's head went from side to side as if she were in great distress. "I gave her . . . I asked her to move that glass." She drew her hands over her mouth.

"So the nurse tells me," said the Deputy rather dryly. "Miss Shepherd held the water glass in her hands for some minutes. Is that true, Miss Shepherd?"

"Malvina asked me to pick up the glass," said Sarah, "to make room for the flowers."

"If you were going to put poison in somebody's glass," said David in a conversational tone, "it would be rather dumb to put your fingerprints on it."

"Or would it?" said Maxwell. "Now, as I see it, these two young ladies were there and no other visitors. Either of them could have put the poison in that glass."

Sarah swallowed. One saw the motion of her throat in this glareless light. "I did not. Whether Malvina did, I don't know. She was with him alone before I came."

"Yes," said Malvina, "but there was no poison in the glass before Sarah came."

"What makes you sure?"

"Why, Edgar drank of it. He was drinking of it, as Sarah came in."

"Is that true, Miss Shepherd?"

"No," said Sarah. "I don't think so. I don't remember that he was drinking out of the glass until just as we left."

"I remember it clearly," Malvina said.

The Deputy had a mouth that lay in a sour arc across the fleshy lower part of his face. He said, "I'm checking for opportunity. . . ." The other man came back at this point and said, "It's there,

161

all right. Just about anything you'd want."

Maxwell nodded. "Now, since I'm looking for opportunity and there seems to be a supply of the poison here, let's see who had a chance to get at it."

Malvina said, "I'm sorry. I'd better tell you." She lifted her face and stared beyond the Deputy into the sky. "This morning when I came with the news that Edgar had survived his fall and was in the hospital, I went to change . . . to dress. My room has a window to the garden. Sarah was supposed to be dressing, too. But I saw her come up through the wall where the steps lead to the laboratory. I wondered . . . but I had to go to Grandfather."

"That is a lie," blazed Sarah. Malvina's face did not lose its mask of painful sincerity.

"Just a minute. . . . Go on, Miss Lupino."

"Grandfather said, and he will remember this and I think Mrs. Monteeth will remember it, too. He said to Sarah that she must take the flowers. That Gust would drive us. And Sarah said, 'Where am I going?' And Grandfather told her she was going to the hospital. And she said, 'Yes. *I do very much want to see Edgar.*' It was a very sudden and vehement thing . . . the way she said it."

Sarah was sitting high on the edge of her chair. "I did say that. I did say it vehemently. I wanted to find out what had happened, why my car went off the road." Sarah's chin was up. "The rest is lies," she stated.

"*Lies*, Miss Shepherd?"

"I did not go to the laboratory. I was not seen coming up those steps because I never went down them. I did not take any poison or have any poison and I did not put any into the glass."

162

"Then Miss Lupino did?" said Maxwell rather slyly.

"For all I know," said Sarah.

Malvina's head went from side to side as if in helpless sorrow.

Maxwell said to his man, "Go ask the servants about this morning."

"Now," he turned upon them sharply, "we have to see what there is in the way of a motive. Even if both of you had opportunity, we can't go very far without a possible motive."

Malvina said drearily, "There wouldn't be any real motive," and her pose suggested pity and sorrow.

"There may have been a motive," said Sarah steadily. "I'm sorry for all of this but I must say it." She was fighting. David watched and admired and lay low. "Something was wrong with my car, I think," said Sarah. "Something had been fixed, some mechanical thing, so that it would go over as it did. *I* was supposed to go over. I wonder if Edgar could have told too much about that if he had stayed alive to tell."

"But he didn't tell," cried Malvina. "He was conscious and he was perfectly well able to tell anything he wished to tell. Why didn't he tell, if there was anything to tell?"

"You were alone with him, Miss Lupino?"

"Yes, yes I was. He . . . Very well," said Malvina, "I see it will all have to come out. For a long time we have all been worried about Sarah. Mr. Wakeley knows this."

"Worried in what way?" asked the Deputy.

"About her mental health," said Malvina. "She had had a good deal of trouble. It seems," said

163

Malvina, "that something dreadful happens every-where she goes."

Sarah's face was white.

"I guess you've heard this before, Wakeley?"

"Yes, I've heard it before," David said shortly. Maxwell had heard it before too, but he hadn't listened when David had tried to tell him. David was watching the little white face and he thought, Better she gets out of here, no matter what. No matter how. A quick yank will be the least pain in the end. He said, "I have suggested that perhaps a psychiatrist . . . But Mr. Fox doesn't seem to think much of the idea."

"Grandfather hates it," said Malvina. "It's old-fashioned . . . but you see, to him it is a disgrace. Yet these things do keep happening. A man was killed in Japan. A date she had. Her husband dropped dead . . ." Malvina began to pour it all out.

Sarah sat still. She wasn't looking at David. She was watching this other man's face, this ordinary man, a sane, a responsible, an unfanciful man.

"Is all this true, Miss Shepherd?" Maxwell asked her without excitement.

"Those things happened," Sarah said, and her tongue moistened her lip. "I . . . don't know why."

"Then," said Malvina, leaning, her forearm on her lap, her hand extended as if to plead, "Mr. Wakeley came here to work on his book. We thought she might be better. But the studio caught fire . . . We don't *know,*" cried Malvina, "we never have known whether these things happened or whether Sarah *wants* them to happen. . . . Edgar tried so hard to help her." Now Malvina was weeping and the tears were real. "Edgar did all he

164

could. But maybe she is getting worse. Maybe she doesn't want to be helped. . . . Maybe . . ."

Sarah said, "It's true I've been . . . followed by these strokes of bad luck . . ." Her voice was about to break and she looked as if she'd crumble.

And David's heart was wrenched to see it but he kept still. He could see something desirable ahead, something looming. Even so, when Sarah pulled herself up and flung back her head, he could have cheered.

Sarah cried out in all their faces, "I would crawl into a hole somewhere and die from the misery of all this, if it wasn't for the lies. When people tell out-and-out lies, I know there's something wrong, and not with me. Miss Lupino is lying to you, sir. And I can prove that."

Maxwell said, "Go ahead."

"Those keys," said Sarah, fighting. "Edgar did keep his lab locked. Since the fire . . . ask the servants . . . he's had a new lock and only one key to it."

"This is the key that was in your pocket?" Maxwell said.

Malvina wept. "Oh . . . Sarah . . ." And Sarah looked at her, startled into silence.

"Considering the accumulation of . . . well, doubt," David spoke quietly, "I think Sarah will be much better off if, under police guard of course, she could be kept in the hospital and competently observed. I think the safest . . ."

Sarah's face flamed. "But *you know* it isn't true," she said, and turned to the Deputy. "I'm trying to explain to you. That key wasn't in the house this morning. It must have been in Edgar's own pocket. I couldn't have unlocked the lab this morning because David brought those keys with him. He can tell you that. He handed those keys to me, not five minutes before you came." Her voice seemed to set the dust motes dancing. In silence they began to fall.

"I'm afraid I don't know anything about the keys," said David Wakeley.

And watched Sarah wilt in her chair, shrink, her spine bending. Maxwell rose. His mouth was flattened to a more cynical arc than before. The man in plain clothes came in. "Nothing," he said to his superior. "The handy man was begging a bite to eat off the Chinaman in the kitchen. They saw nobody. The Missus was with the old gentleman."

Malvina wailed softly, "Grandfather . . ."

David got up and went toward Sarah. He suffered for her, hated it, but he thought, Let them take her away. *Make* them take her away. The police can keep her from being murdered. God knows whether I can. This has priority. This is imperative. She mustn't be murdered, because after that it will be too late for any explanations. He said, "I'm sorry, Sarah. I know you don't understand. If we all think you will be better off . . ."

"Why, I understand," said Sarah and she rose. "I know that Malvina is lying. I know that you are lying. But surely the truth will come out and I am not afraid to go with the police. I didn't poison or try to hurt anyone and that will come out. I don't think I have lost my reason," she said, "but if I have it will be best for me to know it. Do you want me to go now, sir? May I get my toothbrush?"

Maxwell stood rocking, heel to toe. He said, "I am inclined to agree that some lies have been told. However . . ."

David said, "I think a doctor . . ." To rush this, to get it over before she tore his heart out, this little blonde girl.

Malvina whimpered, "Grandfather . . . Oh, Grandfather . . . Oh no . . . He has had so many blows. Fire. Edgar's accident . . . death. If you arrest Sarah for murder, if you take her away, I think he will die."

Sarah said, "That's true," and she brought two trembling hands together.

Maxwell said, "Now, I haven't said I would arrest Miss Shepherd."

"Don't, then," said David sharply. "But surely the hospital . . . Why not tell Mr. Fox she isn't well?"

Maxwell said, "I've been to the hospital. You forget that." He rocked. "I am aware of the fact that the keys were in Dr. Perrott's pocket when he was brought in there. I know to whom they were given and when."

The wind went out of David Wakeley. He saw Sarah's proud little face.

Maxwell frowned at them all. "I know Wakeley was lying. I don't know whether Miss Lupino was lying. I don't know whether Miss Shepherd's emotional stability is all it ought to be. But damned if I don't think she's got guts," said the Deputy.

Sarah said, "Thank you," in that breaking voice. "But I don't think I can stand any more. If I could go to my room . . . I will be there if you want me."

"Lock your door," said David. She looked at him as if he were a mote of dust. Maxwell nodded and Sarah walked across the carpet and into the corridor.

David said harshly, "I want that girl in the hospital."

"Why?" said Maxwell, eying him. "It wasn't very safe for Dr. Perrott."

"With a police guard. With every protection." David felt frantic.

"I'm leaving a man on the gate here," Maxwell said. "Miss Shepherd won't go anywhere that I don't know. Nor will the rest of you."

Malvina said, "I don't think anything more can happen. For my grandfather's sake, I'm grateful. All so terrible . . ."

"May I see the old gentleman?"

Her eyes came up, frank and wide. "He is very much disturbed. He is resting. I wish you could wait until another time."

"Don't want to injure him in any way," the Deputy muttered.

"Thank you."

"We will need a little more light on this affair, which I intend to get. I'm not satisfied with any of you people. Goodbye, for now." Maxwell was leaving.

David cast one black look at Malvina and raced after him.


"For God's sake!" he cried, in the garden.

"Keep your shirt on," Maxwell said.

"You can't leave her here, I tell you. I told you before. The whole thing is a plot against her."

"I don't get that," Maxwell said. He paused, his strong beefy legs apart, and looked off over the wall at the view. "Sarah Shepherd didn't get poisoned. Perrott got poisoned. It's Perrott who is dead."

"Sarah Shepherd will be dead for all you . . ."

"Now hold it. Hold it. I'm not going to arrest anybody on the strength of a lie outa you, Wakeley. Especially when I happen to know it is a lie. I know why you did it. Of course. And love is a wonderful thing but never lie to a cop, Wakeley." Maxwell's face was a rock.

"I would have told you once she was out of here."

"You tell me the truth and all of the truth and no more, ever."

"That was her car that went off the road and it must have been fixed. I'm positive that somebody wanted her to die in it."

"She didn't," said Maxwell, "and we won't know anything about the condition of the car until we can raise it."

"In the meantime . . . what about the meantime?"

Maxwell looked around the garden. "You stick around and keep an eye on her, why don't you? I'm putting a man handy. I've got digging to do."

"Malvina is a liar," raved David. "She'd rather lie . . ."

"That's impossible. Lots of people are liars. I've met a lot of them. But I'm not going to get into any deal where I'm responsible if the old boy dies. Or is Malvina lying about that, too? What's the state of his health? Do you know?"

"Perrott was his doctor." David felt as if he had run into a wall. "The whole house runs on the assumption that he can drop dead. But I don't know."

"Uh-huh," said Maxwell. "Now, you don't want me to drag your Sarah off to jail or its equivalent and have the old man die of the

169

disgrace when you, yourself, don't believe for one minute that the kid is guilty of anything? Or do you?"

"Malvina is guilty. Take her, then. If you want to take the one who poisoned Edgar, take her," begged David. "She did it."

"Did?"

"Obviously."

"Yeah?"

"Why does she lie? Why does she try to put it on Sarah?"

"Well, some people don't think of it as lying when they add on a little bit to bolster up what they've already decided is the truth. Now listen, Wakeley. You don't know everything. What if it's like this? Those two girls go there. His only two visitors. Neither of them did it. So each of them is sure the other one *did*. They believe that."

"Neither of them did it! What . . . ?"

"Ever think maybe Perrott did it himself?"

"What do you mean?"

"So the car might have been deliberately steered off the road by him, for all we know. So the poison belongs to him, don't it? He had access. He must have known it was in that glass. In the last analysis he *took* it. Couldn't have drunk it unaware. Well? Could be he had some hidden in his clothes. Could be he got out of bed and got to it. This is one thing I'll try to check."

"Why would he?"

"Well . . . and this is what you don't know and I do . . . first words Perrott says when he gets conscious, and the nurse was there . . . Perrott says he wishes he hadn't been saved. He'd rather have drowned."

David swallowed.

170

"If what we've got here is a suicide," said Maxwell, "I'm not going to make a fool of myself."

"I hope you're not," said David dangerously.

"You managed to do it," said Maxwell coldly. "And what's more, you are going to have a sweet job squaring yourself with that little blonde." He began to move away.

"Maxwell, did Consuelo McGhee . . . ?"

"Talked to her," Maxwell grunted. "She's a great old gal, Consuelo. I'll tell you right here and now, Wakeley, if it weren't for Consuelo McGhee, I'd crack down on you plenty for lying to me. So you've had one favor out of me, which is my limit. So watch it, willya?"

# Chapter 15

David turned and looked back toward the house. So far in his life he'd had no moment in which he felt so lost, so indecisive, so unfocused upon a course of action. He simply did not know what he was going to do.

Then he saw Malvina come out of the glass door with a harassed, bustling look to her. She moved swiftly toward him. "The arrangements," she said. "They want me to choose. Oh David, will you go with me?"

"Where's Sarah?" His voice cracked with alarm. I'm too jumpy, he told himself. Surely they haven't killed her in these four minutes.

"Sarah's locked in her room. Ah, don't worry, David." Malvina's eyes glistened. "Surely poor Sarah can't do anything . . ." His jaw worked and he stared bleakly down at this liar. "David, I must go to the funeral place. Will you help me?"

"And your grandfather?" He didn't hear what she was asking.

"Resting. I don't think Sarah would hurt Grandfather, anyhow."

He kept looking down at her and controlled his

fury. "I want to talk to Sarah."

"She won't let you in," said Malvina pityingly. "Leave it, David. Mrs. Monteeth is with Grandfather and Gust is here. Won't you please take me to the village? I can't do this sad thing alone. Will they let us go?" She peered beyond him.

David had an idea. He shook himself. He said contritely, "I'm sorry. Of course. I understand. I have to change but first let's ask." He took her arm and hurried her toward the place where the gate had been. Maxwell had not gone yet. He was occupied with stowing into his car a boxful of oddments garnered from Edgar's laboratory. He was instructing his man, who was to remain.

To him Malvina purred out her problem. Must go and choose among caskets. Poor Edgar. Last thing she could do for him. Malvina was both pitiful and brave. She begged prettily. "May David take me?"

Maxwell wasn't charmed and had no pity. He looked sourly at her, as if he were tempted to say "Do it on the phone." David, behind her back, made an outward scooping motion of his palm, which Maxwell may or may not have seen in the tail of his eye. What the Deputy said, in a manner that admitted no arguing, was, gruffly, *"I'll* take you, Miss Lupino."

"But how am I to get back? I need . . . I want someone with me."

"I'll go with you and send you back," the Deputy said. "Wakeley better change before he gets pneumonia. Also, I want Wakeley to stay put." His glance flicked at David. Then Malvina might as well have been in custody. She had to go, as this man was taking her. She cast one look back at David, a strange bewildered look, as if she, also, did not know what she would do now, and implored him to wait . . . to do nothing until she was back in the game.

Jubilant, David raced through the garden and into the guest house, where he changed his clothes in record time. He could break Sarah's door down if he had to. Somewhat cleaner and drier, he came into the house, this glittering lizard of a house, silent, spacious, with nothing but the sky beyond the glass on the seaward side. He raced into the bedroom corridor.

Grandfather's door stood wide open. David was lifting his hand to knock at Sarah's door when Fox called out querulously, "David?"

"Yes, sir." Now he had to turn and concede that Grandfather was there. The old man was not in his bed but ensconced in an easy chair and Mrs. Monteeth was fussing about him. "David, if you please . . ." said Grandfather. "No more. No more. Let the child be. Let us have peace," said Grandfather. His head lolled on the chair back. His hand pressed his breast. "A little time," the old man said, "for all of us to understand and consider our grief. If you please . . ."

David saw Mrs. Monteeth, by the stern warning of her frown, fiercely enjoining him to obey. Could this old man's heart stop? David's hand fell.

"Yes, sir, of course," he said quietly. "I'll do nothing to upset you."

The old man said, "A little peace . . . a little peace in my house . . ."

Back in the big room David chewed his lips. Well, if the old man was watching Sarah's door so could David watch it, he thought. Stalemate? But he thought, No. Because he could go around to the window where the old man couldn't hear and

175

wouldn't see and could talk to Sarah just the same. But how the old man *used* his health. It lay like a threat behind every request and made a request a command.

Another idea struck him and he hurried to the phone.

"Consuelo?" (She was there. How she stood by!)

"Yes, Davey. I've heard about Dr. Perrott. Tell me . . ."

"I haven't time. It's a mess. Consuelo, do you know a doctor?"

"Of course."

"Send him up to the Nest. Call him in my name. No, in Malvina's name. Send him up to look at the old man."

"Is the old man . . . ?"

"I don't know. That's what I want to find out. Tell him the old man's doctor is dead and that he's got a wonky heart, had a shock, looks bad. Tell him it's an emergency."

"Is it, Davey?"

"God knows it is. Edgar's dead and Malvina's out of the house for a half hour at least. If I can immobilize the old man maybe I can get Sarah out of here."

"I'll send him," said Consuelo. "Dr. Haines. Or failing him, Dr. Price. Oh, I'll send one of them arunning."

"Send me one sound honest medical man," said David with a sense of almost weeping relief. He hung up. He wanted to run out-of-doors and around to Sarah's window but he did not. He would stay where he was. Not until the doctor came would he move into the garden.

\*       \*       \*

176

Sarah sat at her desk, writing. She worked carefully. She wrote on the paper words that had to do with death and with the world as it would be after she died. She was making her Will.

This was because she hoped not to be murdered.

The sea sounds were far and rhythmically constant and the ear discarded them. The room seemed so silent, she could hear the pen's touch on the paper. Outside the window on her left there was silence in the garden.

She thought, This is an interlude, a recess in the violence. Edgar was dead. Enough. Enough for a little while. Or did Malvina expect the State to take care of murdering Sarah now? But the Deputy believed nothing yet, neither the truth nor the lies. The bald lies, the black lies, had not prevailed. The truth had not prevailed either. For herself, Sarah would have been happier to have been taken away. But there was more than herself to be considered.

She thought, How could I have been so blind, so stupid, as not to have seen my enemy before?

Malvina was her enemy. Granddaughter of Lupino, that cruel and terrible man. Sarah shuddered and the pen wavered and she snatched at her composure because this handwriting must be even and firm and sane.

This was an interlude, like a hurricane's core, and it would not last. So she must get this document in order. The silence and the false peace and the cessation would not last, because Sarah herself was going to move and break it.

She heard the voices in the corridor, a strange man's voice, loud and hearty. She listened a moment and nodded. Now Grandfather's door would soon close. Her pulse leaped. She steadied her hand. She signed her name to the bottom of the paper.

"Mr. Fox," said David politely, "this is Dr. Price."

"Eh? What's this!" The old man strained back.

"Malvina," said David sweetly, "is only thinking of you, sir. She thought since your own doctor cannot look after you anymore, it was imperative that someone take over."

"I am not prepared . . ." said the old man. He was furious.

"Now, Mr. Fox," said Dr. Price, barging cheerfully to a table and putting his bag upon it, "since I am here, we'll just see."

"Oh, Doctor," said Mrs. Monteeth, "I've been so worried. Not knowing what's best to be done."

"We'll see what's to be done." The doctor was not going to be put off by the patient's surprise. "How are you feeling, sir?"

The old man's face was ugly. His mobile lips opened to reveal the teeth, the stained snags. "Malvina took this upon herself?"

"For your sake," soothed David. He introduced the doctor and Mrs. Monteeth. He backed out and closed Grandfather's bedroom door.

He put his knuckles against the pale wood across the hall. He breathed "Sarah?"

The key rattled. "Will you come in, David?" said Sarah quietly. "I want to talk to you."

He saw no hatred and no shrinking. "Doctor's with your Grandfather," he stammered, stepping in.

"I know. Thank you." That beautiful mouth was curving in a small grateful smile.

"Malvina's gone to the village. Sarah, forgive

178

me." His hands craved to reach out for her but he kept them still. "What I was trying to do . . ."

"Why," she said, "I know."

He felt even the muscles of his eyes relaxing almost sleepily in this relief. "That's wonderful," he murmured.

"I know that you thought I'd be safe if they took me away."

"Sarah . . ." He nearly choked. He thought, This girl! This marvelous girl! We are not going to have any torn female feelings or bleeding hearts!

"You do think she'd been trying to kill me?" Sarah asked steadily.

"Yes, I do."

"So do I," she said.

David's head swam with the relief. But he watched her. He was afraid to believe in this Sarah. He didn't see how she could be as she was. "We can't talk about it now," he said. "We must . . ."

"Yes," said Sarah. "Yes, plans. I want you to help me." Now a little blush came into her face.

"I will," he said, his eyes glowing. "Sarah, are your shoulders burned at all?"

"No. Why?"

"What can I do to help you? Will you let me take you away?"

"If you'll marry me," she said.

He lifted his hands. He put them carefully at her shoulders. Her head tilted backward to see him as he loomed closer. So David put his mouth on hers. He felt its tremble, its sweetness tempted and then withdrawn. He said shakily, "For keeps, Sarah? Or shouldn't I ask?"

"Not . . . yet . . ." she said, as breathless as he. "No, it's a plan. Will you listen, because I've been thinking." He kept one hand on her shoulder.

"About Malvina," said Sarah. "I've tried to understand her. It must be the money. You see, she has a big allowance. But if Grandfather were to die . . ." Her breath was troubled and she stepped back and he let her go.

"Half of the money," she went on, "after taxes . . . won't give her as much as she has now. I worked for an accountant once. I know. I remember. But suppose I died and Grandfather left it all to her. Then it would be enough."

David said, "Yes, I see."

"So she wants me to die before Grandfather dies. And perhaps . . . he is so frail . . . perhaps she wants to hurry."

David didn't say he thought the old man was in it, too. He wasn't even sure of it. He listened gravely.

"And I think Edgar was helping, for a while. But then Edgar decided he couldn't let her go on with it. And he was going to tell. So she . . . had to stop him."

"I think that's a good guess."

"But," Sarah's hands twisted suddenly, "if she managed to get rid of me, then I'm afraid she wouldn't wait."

"Wait?"

"She poisoned Edgar. If she got rid of me," said Sarah, "I think she'd try to get rid of Grandfather, too. And I don't know what's ever to stop her trying, unless the whole thing turns out to be not worth while."

"I think I . . ."

"You see? If I am married and have made my Will, which I have done . . . it's here. I . . . it's all left to you. But I think a husband has a right in the law, besides . . ."

180

"You were once married," he murmured.

"Peter died. A living husband . . . You would have to stay alive."

"I intend to," said David quickly. "But Sarah . . . I don't like to object . . ."

"Go on."

"If you died and your Grandfather were alive, he could and would make *another* will. You can't will to me what you haven't got yet."

"Oh, but Grandfather would do as I wanted," Sarah said.

"You think he would?" David felt he had to be careful. Sarah was fine. Sarah was steady in this plan of hers. But Sarah had had too much.

"Why, Grandfather's fond of me," she insisted, "and of you, too, David. Grandfather would rejoice if . . . if I were married. No, don't you see? This makes it all *useless* for Malvina. It must be so, or why, all this time, have she and Edgar tried to keep me from knowing people, from making friends? And I think it must be so because Edgar *told* me."

"Edgar? *Told* you?"

"At the hospital. Edgar told me to get married. He said it would be safer."

"It could be so," said David slowly in a moment. "You want to marry me, do you, Sarah, to save your grandfather's life?"

"Oh, and mine, too," she said hastily. "I thought . . . Don't you agree?"

David looked down. "I agree," he said solemnly. He batted at his crown. "Now how the dickens are we going to get married?"

"We'll have to fly to Nevada. Or Mexico. I have enough money, if I can cash a check."

He drew his breath in. "Let me take you out of

this Nest right now. I have a friend. She's been waiting to take you in. Come on, quick, while there's this chance. That's the first thing."

"Isn't there someone at the gate?" said Sarah.

"Yes, but . . ."

"Will they let me through?"

"They'll let you through. I'll get you through. They may follow . . ."

"I don't think they will let us fly away to Nevada or to Mexico."

"Well, no," he said.

"Then . . . we have to sneak," said Sarah and her mouth curled. "I was thinking . . ."

David said, stunned, "Just tell me your plan."

"Down the beach way. It's possible. I could get to the highway. You could pick me up. They won't follow you, will they? Nobody thinks you poisoned Edgar."

"No. Nobody thinks that. Come on, then. Now."

"It's not low tide," she said. "I can't swim. I don't see how I can get around the big rock until the tide is out."

"When will it be low tide?"

"I looked it up. I should think I could make it . . . maybe at eight o'clock. Or surely soon after."

Then he sat down. Hands dangling, he thought about it. She'd run away with him and that was good. That was fine. That was his objective. But she must do it *now*.

He said, "Sarah, I want you to come out through the gate. I'm afraid to wait."

"I don't like it, either," she said uneasily. "But if we go through the gate, they could put me in jail or somewhere, where we couldn't possibly get married.''

''You'd be safe.''

''Safe,'' she nodded, ''but . . .''

''Sarah, according to your own figuring, Malvina won't hurt your grandfather while you are *alive*.''

''But it doesn't settle anything,'' she said.

Her hand took the paper. ''Well, anyway,'' she said, ''you'll take this to a lawyer or someone. Maybe it will be enough. I can tell Malvina I've made a Will. I think I can get Grandfather to make it plain that he'd respect my wishes. So . . .'' Her voice was a little dreary. *''Wasn't* I thinking?'' she asked him piteously. ''I thought I was. Was I dreaming it all up, just to get married? Wouldn't it work?''

''Sarah, darling.'' He had her shoulders between his hands again. ''I think it's a wild and absolutely nutty idea that will work like a charm. It's the best idea in the world, for us to get married.'' She leaned forward, her head came against his breast. She leaned there silently and he held her and did not move. He murmured, ''All I wish is that the tide was out.''

''Can you,'' her voice was muffled, ''can you arrange about a plane? Could we get away in one?''

''I know a man,'' he said. ''Private plane. I also know a woman with influence. We could do that. All right, Sarah, just as you say. I'll have Consuelo waiting for you on the highway in her car and she will smuggle you away. Maybe disguise you.''

''It'll be f-fun,'' she said.

''But there's one thing.'' David grew stern. ''You'll go down to the beach while I am *here*. I'll

183

talk to them, keep them busy so nothing can stop you."

"Talk to Malvina?" She stirred in his arms.

"Yes, Malvina. And your grandfather, too." David was afraid. "You won't . . . you'd better not tell him about this. He's had enough excitement."

"I know."

"No one will tell him you have disappeared until . . . until he is able to take it. So there's no need to worry."

"It'll be all right," she said. "He knows. I told him already, that some day, as soon as I could, I'd run away."

David's pulse jumped. "When was that, Sarah?"

"Oh, I don't know. It was after the fire."

*Bet it was*, thought David. He didn't dare ask her if she had planned to run away *in her car*. "Sarah, now I remember what I've wanted to ask you. Where did you get the headache pill?"

"What pill? Oh, the day of the fire? When I fell asleep? Why, Grandfather gave me two of his." She lifted her face. "Edgar knew what they were."

"I . . . see," said David. "I wondered. It seemed odd to me."

He saw. But he didn't know what she would do if he told her. He didn't know how to tell her that the old man was trying to kill her, too. He didn't know *why*. So how could he tell her? She was running away with him, to save the old man. And if he told her, would she run away?

He thought, Oh Lord, no. She's had too much. So he said gently, "Sarah, one thing more."

"Yes?"

"I'm terribly in love with you."

"I don't think . . ." she swayed away, "you can be so sure."

"Well, never mind," said David cheerfully. "We'll just run away and get married. Sarah, don't unlock your door for anyone."

"No."

"Don't eat or drink."

"No."

"Don't . . . stumble going down the path."

"No. No, I won't."

"Don't let anyone suspect. Don't tell a soul this plan."

"Oh no."

"Ah, be careful. But I'll be here until you are safe away." His hand behind him was opening her door. "You start down the beach path at eight o'clock, then?"

"Yes."

"You can get around this rock alone?"

"At low tide, I can."

"I'll have you met or meet you, right away. I'll see about a plane. Don't worry about the fare. We'll try Nevada."

"All right, David."

"They'll marry us in Las Vegas. And then . . ."

"Oh, you forgot. The Will." She ran to get it.

David looked over his left shoulder at Grandfather's closed door. Then over his right, down the corridor toward the big room.

Malvina was standing, not three feet away, against the corridor wall.

# Chapter 16

She didn't move. She looked speechless with anger.

David said nothing. He took the paper from Sarah's quick hand, made a gesture that tried to express hope and good cheer and a need for silence. He closed Sarah's door and heard her lock it.

He took one swift step and got Malvina by the forearm and rushed her, pushed her, simply took her along the corridor and into the big room. She said furiously, "So you're going to elope with little Sarah? What a fool you are! She's not even sane!"

"Shut up," said David. "Listen."

If Malvina had obeyed at that moment, he would have had no words for her to listen to. But Malvina said angrily, "All I have to do is tell the man at the gate and you won't get out of the state, you know. You won't elope."

"Are you jealous?" he insulted.

"No." She whipped the word back with anger.

"Then what's the matter with you? You don't want to get Sarah where she ought to be?" Now he had a glimmering of what he could say. "Don't you think," he said with his hands rough and

187

unkind, "she ought to be in the hands of a psychiatrist?"

"Are *you* a psychiatrist?" she sneered.

"Listen, Malvina, if you can calm down. You and I both lied, trying to convince Maxwell to lock her up somewhere. But he was not convinced, was he? All right. Listen. This elopement is Sarah's idea."

"Sarah's?"

"Yes. Sarah's. So, let her try to run away. Who do you think is going to be waiting for her on the highway?"

"What do you mean? What are you doing?" Her eyes turned. She'd believe in a plot.

"I'm getting Maxwell to wait on that road," he told her.

"But why?"

"Because once she's caught trying to run away, he'll be convinced. Don't you understand?" He shook her, covering with vehemence this desperate scramble for a good lie to tell her. "And don't go running to your grandfather and get *him* excited."

"As if I would!" she cried. "That's what I'm avoiding."

"So am I. Get the point, will you? The quickest and easiest way to get Sarah out of here and let there be peace, is for me to agree to her plan." (Let this double-crosser believe I'm a double-crosser, prayed David, so I can get Sarah safely out of here.)

Malvina leaned back, hanging on the strength in his hands. "I don't believe you," she said contemptuously. "I think you're a romantic. You want to 'save' Sarah," she sneered and he wished he could hit her.

"I don't care what you think as long as you keep quiet," he said. "You know and I know that girl is trouble, isn't she? Doesn't make any difference why. Trouble and tragedy wherever she goes. She is a Jonah. Do you want to get it out of this house and spare the old gentleman? Or don't you?"

"I do. I do. But . . ."

David kept holding her but now the range of his vision, that had been concentrated on her face, widened, and he realized that both Gust Monteeth and Moon the Chinaman were standing in the dining room and listening to all he had been saying. He looked behind him. No, Grandfather was not there, as he had half expected, listening, too, with his head cocked.

"Where's the doctor?" he said. "Gone?"

Malvina's face showed no more than a flicker of the eyes but he had hold of her forearms and to his fingers, through the flesh, came the news of her inner earthquake. He felt the deep shock that hit her, the heart leap, the blood pounding.

"Doctor?" Malvina said with only a faint frown showing on her face.

"I called a doctor to see your grandfather, of course. Wisest thing. Don't you agree?"

Malvina began to stand on her own balance. She tried to pull out of his grasp. "I hadn't thought of it," she said. "Why, of course I agree. That was good of you, David." Her eyes glistened. The smooth mask was closed. But he could feel in his fingers the skip and flutter now, the scared heart trying to swing steady. He let her go.

He said to Gust, "Has the doctor left?"

"Yes sir, Mr. Wakeley. Left a few minutes ago." Gust stepped through the wide opening from the dining room where he and Moon had been doing Mrs. Monteeth's chore, setting the table for dinner. Gust said, "Should I call the man from the gate,

189

Miss Malvina?"

Malvina said, "No, Gust. No. I'll take care of this."

She turned her back on them all and walked toward the fireplace where, as was customary at this pre-dinner hour, a fire had been lit.

David followed her. "You'll do as you please. He's your grandfather," he muttered. Malvina's neck arched as her head went down. "But I thought . . ."

"She wants to elope with you? She asked you to do that? Crude of her."

"Ah," he said, "the poor kid. Doesn't know what she's doing. Better let her go of her own volition, I thought. Who knows what she'd do, if anyone tried to take her away forcibly."

Malvina said, "I think you are in love with Sarah."

"I told you, I'm sorry for her. But Maxwell wouldn't listen to me."

"You didn't try to make him listen when I wanted you to go to the village . . ." Malvina smouldered.

"I had *been* trying," David said. "I knew he wouldn't listen. Don't forget, he thinks *you* may have poisoned Edgar. That's no fault of mine."

Malvina sighed. "Why eight o'clock?" she asked.

"Oh, Sarah says low tide," he muttered. "Well?"

She was rubbing her forearms as if she were cold. "I don't know, David." Now her voice mourned her indecision and she turned to let him see her innocent face.

"Do you think Sarah poisoned Edgar?" David asked her.

"I . . . can't see what else. Since I didn't." She let

her eyes fill with tears and David marveled.

"Don't you want a murderess out of this house?" He stepped closer. "Let her think she is eloping. To get her away."

"You may be right. I . . . must see how Grandfather is."

David took out a handkerchief and gently he dried her eyes. "The old man will surely die," David said sadly, "unless somehow, quietly, the source of all this trouble leaves his house."

"I'm afraid so," Malvina said, tears spilling. "I'm sorry, David. Perhaps I didn't understand. She's . . . unpredictable just now, isn't she? She might do anything. Might even . . ." Malvina shuddered.

"Kill herself?" said David. "Is that in your mind, too?"

"Oh yes, I am afraid. Oh, that would be the end of Grandfather." Her mouth was shaping into her smile! "Thank you for all you are trying to do to help us," she said.

Then she left him and went toward Grandfather's room.

David sat down in the inglenook. House of liars, he thought glumly, and he himself was getting to be as swift and facile a liar as any. Malvina might yet stop the plan. He didn't see why she should. She had worked hard and told lies to get the Sheriff's Deputy to believe Sarah guilty and take her away. She should be tempted by this suggestion. But if, instead, she raised a row . . . why, let her.

He no longer cared if any excitement hurt the old man. He only cared for Sarah and her safety. If Malvina raised a row why he, David, would simply raise it louder. He would then bodily tuck Sarah under his arm and carry her away.

Malvina was thinking of suicide. For Sarah, that is. Malvina was shocked because there had been a doctor. Now what was the reason for that? What could the doctor have seen or found out? Sitting here, David could see down the corridor where no one moved and no one knocked at or entered by Sarah's door. Still, from the telephone, he could see just as well.

Malvina had hidden behind the mask of her face but he had been touching her. He had felt the blood jump. He wondered. *Why?*

So he would telephone the doctor.

"Fool!" said Grandfather viciously. "You have no brains. My son was a fool and he married a fool and a fool was produced of their union."

Malvina knelt by his chair. "Sarah can't go. If she gets away, you know, everything . . . everything could collapse."

"If you would sometimes," the old man's eye was lightning, "do as I say."

"But Grandfather . . ."

"Blunders," he spat at her. "Those lies to the Deputy. Suppose he had taken her off and called a psychiatrist? As no doubt he would. Those people *inquire* into memory and childhood. It is the last thing that must happen to Sarah. What a risk you took and to no purpose. Aaaah, you are a fool!"

"Did you want *me* in jail, then?" she said sullenly.

"You were not in danger. You had done as I said. How did you fail to get David away? *There* might have been a most excellent chance. I still have some of the same poison. And a police officer to witness Sarah in the very mood for guilty suicide.''

"She . . ." Malvina bit her mouth.

"And even David seeming to betray her, or so you told me."

"Sarah wasn't . . . *in* that mood . . .''

"Of course she was," the old man raged. *"Why* didn't you take David to the village? Why did you fail?''

"The man, Maxwell, made me go with him. What could I do?"

The old man glared. "And above all, now, in this crisis, you make the colossal blunder. You send me a doctor!"

"No. No, I did not. It was David who sent him."

"You are lying, Malvina." He was evil and furious. "Don't tell your stupid lies to me."

"Am I mad!" she whispered, in her eyes the only truth of her life, her wish for this old man's approval. "Did he see . . . ?"

"Of course, he saw. How could a doctor examine me and not see my scar?"

"Did he ask . . . ?"

"Yes, yes, of course. I told him how I fell on the rocks, as we faked it. And how Edgar and the Neppers took care of me. Aaaahh," the old man made a sound of deepest disgust, "blunders, blunders. And Mrs. Monteeth saw it, too, and David permitted to do such a thing!"

"Can anything be done, Grandfather? If Sarah elopes with David, who is a friend of Consuelo McGhee. And the doctor has seen it. It will all pull together."

"I know. I know," the old man said. "Don't tell *me* what danger we are in!"

"Even if he isn't lying to me, if he intends to give

her to the police . . . then a psychiatrist . . ."

"I know." The old man's eyes were cold. "The solution is what it always was, Malvina. Without Sarah, we are in no danger. Without Sarah, there is nothing to fear."

"What shall I do, Grandfather? Tell me what to do."

Grandfather brooded.

"We have until eight o'clock. Isn't there some poison?"

"Poison," said Grandfather. "Oh yes. Buried in the border along the sea walk. Or I might have put it in her breakfast coffee. *You* told me the police would search this house. Another of your blunders."

"Shall I get it?" She half rose.

"No," he said.

"No?"

"You are to do nothing."

*"Nothing?"*

"When I told you my plan, you sent Edgar off in Sarah's car." He was like a sulking child.

"I had to."

"Do as I say," he snarled, "if you can do anything so easy and simple. Tell Sarah I am better. I am coming to dinner. Tell David to join us. Sarah must come to dinner, too. All must be as usual."

Malvina now rose to her feet. "Yes, Grandfather," she said dubiously. "But how will you poison Sarah and not be in danger?"

"What I will do I will not tell you," he said angrily. "Do nothing, Malvina."

Someone rapped on the door. "Who is it?" Gibberish answered. "Ah, Moon. Yes, come in."

The Chinaman entered with a tray. "No tray,"

said the old man. "I have changed my mind. Tell Mrs. Monteeth I shall be at table. Cocktails? Yes, it is nearly time."

The Chinaman bowed. He backed out and closed the door.

"Now do as I say," said Grandfather to Malvina. "And you are not to think. Go at once and tell Sarah."

"Will you let her go?" said Malvina throatily. "You are old. For you it is not so important. Sarah loves you. That was your insurance. Don't you care what happens to me?"

"Thinking?" he said nastily. "I'll think for us both, if you will allow me. Now I wish to be alone for at least fifteen minutes. Can you manage that?"

"Yes, Grandfather." Malvina's face grew innocent.

"Then we shall meet by the fire, as is our custom."

Behind her mask the tortuous thoughts were working. She assumed he was going to go forth in these fifteen minutes to retrieve the poison from its hiding place. "Suicide?" she murmured. "She could easily be put in the mood for it. If she knew that David was planning to betray her . . ."

"You haven't the cleverness," said Grandfather contemptuously. "Leave it alone, Malvina. And leave me, now."

Malvina's nostrils quivered. "Oh, I understand," she murmured. She left him.

The old man got out of his chair. He tightened the sash of his brocaded coat. He stepped into the study. From there he stepped out to the sea walk. He bent over the foot-wide strip of soil along the wall but he did not touch the soil where the little bottle lay buried. He grasped a plant supporter, a circle of heavy wire with four wire legs, and he pulled it from the soft earth. He pulled up a second one, also.

Then he walked briskly past the windows of his own bedroom and with no glance toward Sarah's windows which lay beyond the upper end of the beach path, he started down. It was dinner time. The coast was emptied of people. Had he been seen in his dark coat from a distance, he might have been anyone. The old man gave no furtive glances behind or below him.

He was out of the range of any eyes at the house level when he stooped and, working hard, pressed and strained to thrust the sharp wire legs of the plant supporter into the hard soil of the path. It was not easy but with effort he succeeded. The wire contraptions were firm enough to surprise a descending foot. And they were placed strategically. Whoever went down the path in dusk or darkness now would doubtless fall. And fall over.

Below, the surf attacked and the rocks resisted in their eternal opposition.

The old man dusted his palms and ascended the path. He walked past the narrow flower border without glancing down. His mouth was wolfish, showing the teeth. Odd that Malvina was such a stupid girl, when Lupino had always been so clever.

# Chapter 17

Phone to ear, David rolled his eyes. The Chinaman was standing in the corridor, down beside the old man's door. He stood irresolute, or so it seemed, which was odd because Moon was nothing if not spry, energetic, direct and impatient.

In his ear Dr. Price said, "Hello?"

"Wakeley, Doctor. Excuse my calling you at home. But I missed speaking to you after you had seen Mr. Fox."

"You weren't around."

"Sorry, sir. How did you find the old gentleman?"

"I want him to come to my office for further exploration."

"But can you tell us," David tried to wriggle around the professional caution, "what care he should have?"

"Superficially, the heart seems sound enough. Suggest taking it easy until we learn more." The doctor was rather abrupt, almost antagonistic.

"Nothing alarming then?"

"Not so far as I find in a preliminary look. Like

to make a more thorough check . . ."

"Did he agree, sir? Did he suggest a time?"

"Said in a day or two." David could sense a certain resentment.

"Is that safe?" he demanded.

"I think so," the doctor said, almost dryly.

"Thanks." David hung up the phone. So, he thought triumphantly, Grandfather's wonky heart is a lie, too! Dr. Price hadn't said so and wouldn't say so, until his examinations had become exhaustive. Yet David could feel the man's annoyance. It would be annoying to be called to attend a man on the verge of disaster and find that the trouble was either not obvious or not there. Oh yes, Edgar had been useful in this house, David thought. The old man's frailty was a legend and an instrument. But an instrument to what? Could it have been this and only this that had made Malvina so startled to hear about a doctor? David wasn't satisfied. He thought of Consuelo. Consuelo could pump the doctor if anyone could.

He wanted to call Consuelo, but he hesitated, wondering if he dared from this phone. He was not unobserved. Mrs. Monteeth was in the dining room now. Gust came, carrying a tray into the big room. The Chinaman came trotting past on his way to the kitchen, head down, muttering to himself.

David moved away from the phone. He sat down uneasily in the inglenook. Malvina came out of Grandfather's door and rapped on Sarah's and spoke to the wood. Then she came in her swaying walk toward him.

She said with her frank smile, "Grandfather feels very much better. He is coming to dinner. You must dine with him, David, and so must

Sarah. Excuse me if I speak to Mrs. Monteeth? Oh, I see Gust has already fetched the cocktails. Good. Grandfather will be with us in a moment. He wants everything to be as usual."

David, with the feeling of dismay about Sarah, felt also rebellion against the pressure of the legend. He said flatly, "I spoke to Dr. Price. He found nothing alarming."

"So Grandfather tells me," Malvina said smoothly with not the slightest sign of alarm. "We are so glad. That's why he feels so much encouraged." She went on by.

David sat in the inglenook, ticking off in his mind the time remaining to be endured—here, where nobody told the truth and he did not even have the slightest idea why they did not. And Sarah was coming to dinner, obedient because Fox must be indulged—impressed by the legend. And Edgar had died of poison.


They were cozily gathered together and the draperies were drawn across the sea side to shut the wild dark world away. Grandfather sat on his cushions, his small feet just reaching the floor. Sarah, in aquamarine cotton, the white bandages on her arms looking quaintly like huge cuffs, sat beside David on the cushioned seat across from Fox. Malvina, in her pale flowing gown of some beige stuff, sat on her stool facing the fire.

Grandfather was talking about old times. He was telling about a Fox and Lupino skit involving a bicycle and a string of sausages. His head dipped and turned and his eyes were merry. His voice chirruped with mirthful memory.

David had to concede that, if you discounted the

fact that all this was taking place in the evening of the day when a member of this household had been cruelly done to death by poison, this recounting *was* comical. The old man evoked the brisk slapstick of the past. Even the timing, essence of comedy, he conveyed to them by his slashing gestures.

Malvina was laughing. Even Sarah smiled. David himself had to concede a chuckle.

"Ah, yes," said Grandfather, wiping an eye, "we were clever."

"They were," said Malvina reverently. "They were very great in those days."

"Everyone says they were great artists," said Sarah fondly. "I can't remember them too well. How I wish I could."

"You've seen them on the stage, Sarah?" David asked.

Grandfather spoke, as Sarah nodded. "If it is an art to face an audience, to start its laughter, to hold it, balloon it, and set them all helplessly rocking . . . yes. Then we were artists." Fox met David's stare. "But it is merely a clever trick, David," he said surprisingly.

"I know very little about how it's done," David said cautiously. "I would certainly call it an art, sir."

"Clever," said Grandfather, sighing. "And my dear old Lupino . . . ah, yes, he was the cleverer of us two." The words fell. There was silence and Grandfather stirred restlessly. "How *he* could dazzle them! Eh, Malvina?"

"He used to be very clever," Malvina said rather evasively.

"Now, then. A toast!" Grandfather raised his glass. His sharp eyes rallied them all. David watched Sarah's fingers move toward her glass. He reached over and took it. He handed her his own. He explained nothing. No one missed what he did. No one mentioned it. Malvina's face was serene and innocent. The old man's glass sailed upward. "To Arthur Lupino!" he cried and ducked a salute and drank the toast.

As David sipped tentatively, gingerly, barely at all, he knew Sarah was scarcely wetting her lips either. Her face was thoughtful. In a silence, only the fire muttered, eating the logs.

Then Sarah lifted her glass higher. "May I give us a toast?" she said. "To Bertrand Fox!" She put the glass to her mouth.

The old man did not drink. He had drained his already. He sank his chin on his breast. Perhaps he was lost in the past.

Malvina clicked her glass down. "I think," she said rather acidly, "dinner is waiting."

"Is it so?" said Grandfather dreamily. "Malvina, you ought not to rush us, my dear. You ought not to be impatient. However . . ." He began to wriggle off the cushions and Malvina helped him.

David slipped his hand under Sarah's arm. As she rose she slid her glass to the low table close against the shaker. It was quite full. She had not taken any. David's fingers congratulated her arm.

They paraded to the table.

David thought, Now, how is it that we go in to dinner, fearing poison? I fear it for Sarah, from either of them. Sarah fears it from Malvina. But Malvina? Is she waiting for it, from the old creature? What if I said so? Gust would soon throw me out. And what would Sarah do then? She would let Gust throw me out. Sarah believes in the legend, still, that the old man could drop dead.

How can anyone believe it, thought David——
watching him quite merrily survive fire and
destruction, crash and suspense, rescue and mur—
der? And now lick his lips over his ancient
cleverness? And relish remembered power? This
evil old clown.

Distaste and fright made David queasy. He
thought, Now *there* is a legend. The grotesque,
wide-lipped, white-painted clown's face is no
child's delight. Not naturally. A child would
scream. If it hadn't been taught a legend, a child
would be afraid.

So they were seated, four. David facing Malvina
Fox facing Sarah. Mrs. Monteeth came to serve
them.

David spoke suddenly. "Sarah, has anyone told
you? There was good news. The doctor thinks Mr
Fox is in very good health."

"Oh!" She looked radiant. "Oh, Grandfather!
How wonderful to hear that!"

The old man cocked his head. His eyes met
David's. "It leads me to wonder if Edgar was no
somewhat too cautious," he said with a nibbling
roll of his lips. "And it leads me to think of quite a
different future. Travel, eh? This place, you see,"
Grandfather shrugged, and then settled his shoul
ders, "has been in a way, beautiful though I find it
somewhat of a prison."

"Not after today," Malvina said. "Sarah, will
you have the dressing?"

"How impatient you are," said Grandfather
"Come, Malvina, can we not take our leisure. Her
we are at dinner and the night before us."

"Will you go back to England, sir?" asked
David.

"Oh, I am spoiled, you see." Grandfather sighed. He put a fork daintily to the salad greens. "All this luxury, eh? Sarah, my dearie, if you have had the dressing . . . I can't see over the flowers."

"Shall I remove them, Grandfather?" said Malvina rather eagerly.

"Malvina, do not fuss," he said crossly. "Just do not touch anything unless I say so."

"England," said Sarah, "must be rather a gray place."

"Too gray. Too gray."

Dessert. Coffee. Malvina increasingly stony-eyed.

They had not eaten. Sarah across the flower centerpiece from Fox was able to seem to nibble but take nothing. David could not eat and had only pretended. Malvina's plate had gone no less untouched.

Now Moon invaded the dining room. He was breaking custom. The old man bridled. Moon let out a stream of his mysterious syllables. He was obviously belligerent and the old man did not awe him.

Sarah said, "I think he wants to know what was wrong with the food. His feelings are hurt. He says we haven't eaten."

Fox said, "Nonsense. It was all delicious." *He* had dined well and heartily. "Your place is not here, Moon."

Moon muttered, swept them all with an angry glance and flounced away. Sarah's eyes widened and then she smiled.

"Sarah, my dearie," said Grandfather curiously. "How is it that you seem to understand him?"

"I didn't realize I could," she said. "But if I

listen carefully . . . Perhaps he knows some Japanese and knows that I do. Or perhaps the languages are alike. I don't know. At least, I do get some of his meaning."

"What was it he said that made you smile, dearie?"

Sarah bit her lip. "Grandfather, I hate to tattle. He called you a name. Not a very bad one."

"Why, the rascal!" said Grandfather. "Eh? All these years, eh?" The old man was laughing. His lids hid his eyes. His teeth were bad. "An independent character is our Moon, eh? What was the name?"

"Oh, something like fraud or thief. Just a cross word, Grandfather."

"He is a good cook," the old man said. "Sarah, my dearie, hadn't you eaten?"

"Enough." Sarah smiled.

"Take your coffee, do." The old man spoke sharply. Sarah put the delicate cup up to her mouth, the coffee that Malvina had poured.

David watched Malvina.

All the while between him and Sarah he could feel the strong bond. She was aware and he was watching and they were (sitting politely at table, chatting, smiling) close and together. Sarah did not really drink the coffee and nothing happened.

Grandfather began to push away from the table. "Come, now. I have not been forbidden. So we shall try a taste of brandy."

He trotted toward the fire.

David looked at his wrist.

Sarah said, at once, "Grandfather, may I be excused? I am really very tired." She looked tired, suddenly, and sad.

"Eh? Why to be sure, dearie." The old man was casual.

David watched Malvina.

Malvina said, "Brandy, Sarah?" It came hissing through her teeth.

"No, thank you." Sarah was graceful. She bent and kissed Grandfather's brow. "Good night. I am so happy you are better."

"I, too," he said. "Good night, little Sarah."

David said "Good night," hardly keeping out of his voice the love and the excitement he was feeling. Sarah smiled and left them.

David sat down hard. "Malvina . . ."

"Just a moment, David?" She turned her back. To hide her face? She took a few steps back toward the dining room, murmured and nodded to the housekeeper. Then she stood with her back turned just a moment too long. But when she faced around, her smile was innocent, her mask was in place.

"Mr. Fox," said David urgently.

"Eh? What's that, David?"

"I am very much worried about the Sheriff's office," David said in a hushed close conspiratorial tone. "This man, Maxwell, has it in his mind that Edgar poisoned himself."

He had caught their attention. He didn't care what he was saying. He was talking for time. Time for Sarah to get out her window and go through the gap in the wall and creep cautiously down to the tiny beach and wade around the big rock and so be free.

Malvina knew she was doing all this, even now. Malvina sat on the stool and her gown fell in all grace but her body was rigid. She did not move or speak. The old man might or might not know what Sarah was doing, and if he knew he might or might not believe that the police would be waiting for Sarah. And might or might not care. He did not move, either. He listened with his head cocked. His hands were still.

No one, of course, waited yet for Sarah. David could not call Consuelo until he himself was away from here. But he would not go, he would hold these two until Sarah had time.

"So, you see," David was saying urgently, "that is why he didn't feel ready to arrest anybody. But . . ."

"Poor troubled Edgar," Grandfather said. "I cannot believe it. Poor troubled little Sarah . . . You say this man told you?"

David talked. The fire muttered. Time went by.

Sarah threw on her short coat, put her purse in her pocket, gently opened the lower sash of the garden window. She got over the sill quickly and sped through an arc of the garden to the opening in the wall. She came out upon the cliff edge and went carefully along the walk to her left. The glass door at the corridor's end opened upon the top of the path. She did not think that from the far fireside Malvina could see her slip quickly down.

To run away . . . to run away with David! She was excited but she meant to be cautious. Her high heels. . . . She would have to wade anyhow. She put one hand on the house wall and the other to her shoe.

"Miss Sarah?" The voice was so close, so loud, so startling, that she trembled. "That you, Miss Sarah?"

"Mrs. Monteeth!" The woman was standing

quietly beside the corridor door. "What are you doing?"

"I was sent to ask you, would you go to Mr. Fox's study and wait on him a minute," said the housekeeper in her prim obedient voice. "Before you run off." Her voice was obedient to someone's instructions, as if Mrs. Monteeth hardly knew what the words meant and had not inquired.

"Grandfather wants me?"

"Your grandfather wants to say goodbye."

"Oh, of course,' said Sarah. She thought, He's so clever! He must have guessed! Oh, I must tell him what David and I are going to do. Tell him I won't be alone. He will be glad.

"Of course," she repeated. "Thank you." And so Sarah walked along the house, on the cliff edge, passing the path, not going down.

The door to Grandfather's study was not locked. She slipped in. The small hexagon was dark. She turned on no light. She sat on the edge of Grandfather's chair and looked out through the glass at the dim beauty of the world, the sparkle of men's lights in their dwellings, the stars and the glimmer of their presence on the sea. Goodbye to the dear old man, and then away. Tide was going out. The way around the rock would be getting easier. She had time.

Then away. With David close to her. Sarah dreamed. It seemed to her, as it does seem to lovers, that all this had been written. They would be together, she and David Wakeley, because . . . There was no word for the cause, although it was as old as all the stars.

\*      \*      \*

Mrs. Monteeth went back into the house, as Miss Malvina had told her to go, not by the corridor but back through the garden again. The next duty on her list lay in the kitchen and Mrs. Monteeth went there.

David in the living room looked at his watch. She had had plenty of time, David judged. Now, he thought, he could go.

# Chapter 18

David drew his remarks to a conclusion. He felt, he said, that someone must check closely on what the police were thinking and doing. He felt he would like to be excused. He would like to run down into the village where he would glean what he could. He was pretending, of course, that he could not imagine Malvina would have told the old man anything.

Neither Malvina nor the old man attempted to dissuade him. Grandfather sat by the dying fire, his face thoughtful, his head nodding, his breath sighing from time to time.

Malvina rose, as if released, and walked with David to the garden door. She stepped outside as he did.

David stood with his ears sharpened. Within the curl of the low house, air in the garden did not stir. The enclosure was breathless and still. At the gate end nothing could be seen. The man on guard was below the garden level. Lights to the right shone in the kitchen. Moon and Mrs. Monteeth could be seen moving in there. Light shone in the Monteeth's bedroom, tail of the house on that eastern end. Gust was there. His shadow moved against the blind.

To the left, in the bedroom wing, Malvina's windows and Sarah's beyond them were all dark. David went swiftly to the left, passed the dark windows, and leaned through the gap in the wall. Nothing could be heard but the sea, booming and crashing.

Malvina said impatiently in his ear. "She's gone. And what am I to tell Grandfather, pray tell me?"

"Nothing, until morning."

"Will you let me know what happens? You *are* going to the Sheriff's office?"

"I'll let you know," he said. "Go in, Malvina. Better stay with him."

"Yes, I will, of course. I hope . . ." Her manner softened. "David, now I think you have been wise."

"I'm glad," he said dryly. He struck off swiftly now to the right, toward the steps.

Malvina stood with her ears sharp. She heard a voice, and David's answer it. Malvina looked where the lights burned and checked again that the three servants were there. She waited, listening for David to go.

The guard was sitting in Edgar's closed car. He opened the car door. "Who's there? Mr. Wakeley?"

"Going to town. O.K.?"

The guard said, "You're alone?" David stood, feeling as if he turned his pockets inside out for inspection. Evidently the guard could see in this light well enough. He said, "O.K."

In Consuelo's Ford, David drove down the switchback road, proceeding slowly and carefully, and then through the Cove, whipping up speed.

At the gates of the Colony, a wavering flashlight stopped him.

"Who's this?"

"Wakeley. Guest at Fox's place."

"Evening, Mr. Wakeley. Alone in the car?" The flashlight dipped into the tonneau.

"What's the idea?"

"Just a minute, sir. Keys to your trunk, please?"

"Oh, for—!"

"Sheriff's orders."

"That so?" David took the keys out of the ignition.

"Supposed to check on who leaves from Fox's place. Listen, a man died this morning."

"Go ahead," said David wearily.

He was delayed only a few minutes but in that time he realized that a shadow detached itself from the porch of the small building from which the guards operated and where by day the agent for Colony Cove properties did his business. When, finally, he drove out into the highway, David knew he was being followed.

Well, then, he could not go for Sarah himself. He must send Consuelo.

David parked abruptly, saw the following car conquer surprise, grinned, rushed for the phone in the drugstore.

"Consuelo?"

"Yes, Davey?" Her voice was as warm and cheerful as ever.

His throat felt full with a rush of gratitude for the existence of Consuelo McGhee. "You know where the highway runs close to the shore, the north end of Fox's place?" he said to her.

"Not the Cove, Davey? The other side?"

"That's right. The highway. Go there, Consuelo. Like the darlin' you are. Sarah's gone down to the little private beach they've got. It's low tide so she'll wade around the rock and make for the highway. You pick her up, Consuelo darlin', and take her to your house. She knows. She'll expect you. We're running away."

"Davey, where are you?"

"Drugstore. I got out through the Cove but the police aren't going to let her fly off with me to Las Vegas."

"Davey!" Her voice squeaked.

"That's right. We're going to elope."

"Aaah," she said, "that's the stuff!"

"Consuelo, be careful. Get her through the town. I don't want the police to pick her up. I don't want her anywhere but with you. I'd go for her myself but I'm followed. Go right away, Consuelo darlin', because she's waiting, poor kid."

"Right away. Davey, you'll come to my house?"

"I've got an errand. I'll give you time, because I'm followed. Then I'll come."

"On my way," Consuelo said staunchly. "I'll get her. Don't you worry."

Consuelo hung up her phone, fluffed at her hair in automatic preparation, reached for her coat. Her mouth was firm in her soft old face. Her eyes were bright and enchanted. Her heart was going a little too fast for one who was sixty-two.

David looked out through the glass of the phone booth. His shadow was not inside the store. He dropped in another coin.

"Dr. Price?"

"Yes. Who is this? Wakeley? Now what is it?"

"Making sure you are home. Coming over to talk to you, Doctor. It may be more important than you know."

212

"About Fox? Absolutely nothing more I can tell you." The doctor was exasperated.

"There is something," David insisted. "I'll be there in ten minutes."

"Now, see here, I can't . . ."

"Wait for me," said David. "It's connected with murder."

"*What* is?"

"That's what I want to find out. Explain when I see you."

"Murder!" the doctor said in plain amazement.

But David hung up. Then he hesitated. He should, he had promised to arrange about a plane. But he thought he could do that from Consuelo's house, where a strategy of their flight would have to be planned. Now, he would go and talk face to face with Dr. Price. Something had made Malvina's pulse leap. And the old man kept a tame doctor, a doctor whose practice had left him because of some doubtful thing, a doctor dependent upon the old man's providence. *Why?*

Let his shadow follow to the doctor's. No harm in that. Meantime, Sarah could be saved. So he left the drugstore, checking out of the corner of his eye on that dark car that waited. . . .

In Grandfather's study Sarah was still dreaming in the dark, when at last the door opened. She turned her head and saw his small figure against the light, knowing that light fell upon her and her loving smile.

Grandfather stood perfectly still.

"Close the door," she said softly. "Malvina mustn't know."

The door closed in a slow sweep. She knew he was coming nearer. "Oh, sit down, Grandfather." He got into his chair and she knelt to be near. She

213

couldn't see his face. She could tell that his breath was short. "You shouldn't have hurried," she chided fondly, "I have time. Now, how did you know I was running away? Do you always know everything, Grandfather?"

He didn't speak, although his hand reached for hers. Sarah clung to the dry old fingers. "I'm glad to be able to say goodbye," she whispered. "I wanted you to know, anyhow. I'm not running away alone, Grandfather."

"Are you not, dearie?" Now he spoke and his voice was a little strange. She could sense some kind of storm in him and she was concerned.

"David and I are going to be married."

"Is that true?" Now his hand squeezed and he sighed wheezily.

"I am going by way of the beach. But of course you *know!* Now how did you know to send Mrs. Monteeth to stop me?"

"Eh, dearie?"

"Oh, I suppose Gust was waiting to stop me if I had gone by the gate?"

"Just so," he said.

But suddenly Sarah was afraid. Now she wished she had not come back into the house, that she had silently gone, that this scene had never begun. She didn't know how to talk to him, how many of her suspicions to tell him. She clung to his hand and said fearfully, "Malvina won't come in here, will she? I'm afraid she *will* stop me. The Monteeths won't tell her? Oh, no, of course they won't. They are loyal to *you.*" She felt him stiffen. "Oh, Grandfather, I don't want to leave you with Malvina. It frightens me. Am I wrong to leave you?"

"No," he said. "No, Sarah. Don't be afraid. You

are right to go."

"She can't . . . Grandfather, if I marry . . ." Sarah put her head against his knee. "In a way it is all for you," she murmured. She didn't want to explain all that she was thinking about his money. It seemed cruel to do so. Sarah was sorry and confused.

"But my dearie," said Grandfather suddenly. "You cannot go by the gate."

"No, because there is a police guard."

"Yes. Yes, I understand." Now he was strong and eager. "Ah, goodbye, dear Sarah. You must hurry, eh?"

"Yes. Yes, I must hurry." She felt released. "Grandfather, you know how I thank you for everything. You are glad I'm going with David? You don't mind?"

"My blessing," Grandfather said solemnly, in the dark. "There, dearie. You know you have it. And now you can hurry, do."

Sarah got to her feet. "I have only to run down the path."

"You are young," he said cheerfully. "You can go nimbly, eh?"

The door flew open. Light washed in. It bathed the old man, showed him bent into his chair, chin down. His head rolled to one side. The eyes turned sideways.

"Sarah," said Malvina sharply. "You are walking into a trap. Tell her, Grandfather." She was tall and imperious.

"What should I tell her?" Grandfather said in a strange voice. "How stupid you are, Malvina! What is this fuss? Now, let her go."

"I'm going," Sarah said resolutely.

"Then I'll tell her," Malvina cried, "how she's

been made a fool of." She let go of the door and bent forward, speaking angrily. "David has gone to the police. He told me so. You think he is going to be waiting for you? Oh no, Sarah—the Sheriff's man will be waiting for you. And catch you running away. *That's* David's plan."

"I don't believe you," Sarah said.

"Then we'll ask Gust, who heard him say so. We'll ask Moon. Everyone heard him say so." Her voice rang. Malvina moved and left a path through the door.

"Except me," said Grandfather, and then loudly, *"except* me, Malvina, from all this nonsense." He lay back in the chair, hand on his heart. "Leave me," he said piteously.

Sarah believed the old man's health was feeble. It had been told her for months, shocked into her by Malvina in the first place. The vague news that some new doctor had been encouraging was all forgotten. She said, in distress, "Oh, Malvina, how could you?" She bent over him, frightened. "Grandfather, can I get your medicine? What can I do?"

"I will get the medicine," Grandfather said. "Just leave me."

"I can't. Oh, what must I do? I *can't* run away."

"Perhaps not," he said. "Perhaps not just now, Sarah. There, dearie. We must only see what new plans to make, eh? Now a moment to be quiet . . ."

Malvina said, victoriously, "Come into the other room, Sarah. Let me prove to you that David Wakeley is a liar."

"You can't do that," said Sarah. "You should know better. Oh, forgive us, Grandfather. Excuse us. *You* mustn't worry."

"No, dear Sarah," said Grandfather, sighing. 'I

shall not."

Sarah walked into the living room. Malvina closed the study door.

Grandfather, his face furious and evil, squirmed out of his chair. He opened the door again, just slightly. He stood there, listening, grimacing, his one hand beating against the darkness.

# Chapter 19

Consuelo pulled off the highway, far out upon the dirt shoulder. She set her brakes and got out of the car. The night breeze was chilly. She drew her coat collar closer to her throat and peered along the strand. She could see no one there, anywhere. Consuelo walked out upon the beach.

On her left cars whipped past, seeming to be monsters traveling at fantastic speeds, and the repetition of their noise, like a man-made surf, and the swift change from headlight to dark to headlight, was confusing. But her vision grew sharper until she could distinguish the great boulder at the far end of the arc of sand. Consuelo began to walk on the sand toward that boulder.

Looking up, she could see the dark tail of Fox's house, and a dark gleam, as if the glass caught some light from the night sky. There was a faint glow at the front of the house but while she was walking it faded away. Consuelo was stout and long un-used to exercise and the going on the sand was heavy. The flickering ribbon of lights on the highway receded and was farther and farther off on its own tangent. Here where she trudged a true night fell.

"Sarah?" she called to the night wind. But now on her right the sea crashed. The white crescents advanced, disintegrated.

Consuelo came to the great rock and stood watching the sea as it delicately danced and imperceptibly, arabesque by arabesque, retreated.

"Sarah? Sarah Shepherd? Sarah?"

Consuelo might have been a bird crying. No human answered.

Sarah ran toward the kitchen calling. "Mrs. Monteeth!"

"Wait a minute." Malvina was behind her. "Sarah, you little fool! Did you think he would marry you? Why, he's got girls of his own. He's driving some woman's car. She lives down the shore. He goes to see her. You don't know *anything*. You're living in a dream. He thinks you're crazy. He's been nagging us all to get a psychiatrist. He *knows* you set that fire and burned up his work."

"No," said Sarah. "No, he does not." She wobbled into the kitchen, leaned against the cupboard.

Gust came out of the Monteeths' room and there they all stood. Moon beside the sink looking over his shoulder with a gleaming eye; Mrs. Monteeth grasping the kitchen counter, her sense of decorum and order outraged, her face stupid with surprise; and Gust, feet apart, waiting for a clue to his duty in this strange matter. Malvina was blazing with her argument and Sarah kept one shoulder against the cupboard as if she were at bay.

"Gust," cried Malvina commandingly. "Tell

220

Miss Sarah. Didn't David Wakeley say he was going to the police? You heard him. Tell her."

"That's right," Gust said. "We heard him all right. He said you had to be got out of the house. He said you was trouble and tragedy. He said let you think you was running away with him. Said he's afraid they couldn't take you by force without a row."

"By . . . force . . ." Sarah's head went back against the wood.

Now Mrs. Monteeth was nodding. The Chinaman had turned to watch.

"Thought it was a dirty trick, myself," Gust said somewhat indignantly.

"But . . . he was lying," gasped Sarah.

"That's what I told you." Malvina's lips were cruel. "Of course he was lying. This crazy idea of getting married! Don't you think an intelligent man picks a wife a little less hectically? Don't be a fool, Sarah. Unless you *are* crazy. Now come back in here and think it over."

"You don't want me to run away." Sarah forced herself to stand free of the support.

"I don't *care,*" Malvina said. "Frankly, I didn't think it was such a bad idea. I'm weary of all this uproar. And besides, I think it's very possible you poisoned Edgar." Malvina's teeth were very fine, and all showing. The servants held their breaths. "Are you determined," said Malvina, "that everyone will suffer? Something terrible *must* happen to everyone around you? David, Edgar, now Grandfather, then me? Maybe the Monteeths too. Are you so haunted?"

Sarah raised her fists. *"Why* didn't you let me go? *Let* them arrest me, then."

"I don't know," Malvina said. "I suppose I'm

sorry for you, Sarah.''

''Listen,'' Gust said. ''Not *that* dirty trick, Miss Sarah. We're all sorry.''

''Sorry,'' echoed Mrs. Monteeth.

''You. . . .'' Sarah was shaking with anger. Her throat closed. Her hands shook. Even her vision was affected. Her lips formed ''David,'' but she had no voice to say it.

''She looks as if she's having a *fit*,'' Malvina said cruelly. ''Of course, she was crazy about him.''

Gust said, ''Can'cha do something, mother?'' and Mrs. Monteeth moved. ''Now, Miss Sarah, poor lamb. Gust says he's just a traitor and that's what he is, that fine Mr. Wakeley. And don't you break your heart.''

''I . . . I won't,'' said Sarah forcing her throat open. ''Oh, I won't. I don't believe it.''

Gust said, ''He was tricking you so's it would look like you wanted to run out on the police, Miss Sarah. Honest, he said so. We all heard it.''

''Yes, I . . . believe that he said so.''

Malvina said, ''She looks terrible. Watch her. I've got to see about Grandfather.''

''You . . . you'll kill him!'' shrieked Sarah.

''You'll manage to do that,'' Malvina said nastily. ''Unless you listen to people.''

''Ask . . . ask Grandfather,'' said Sarah pitifully, ''what I am to do.''

''Yes. I will ask him,'' Malvina said.

Mrs. Monteeth had a strong arm around Sarah, and Sarah sagged upon it. ''Because I don't know what to do,'' she said, ''what to do . . .'' The sense of evil and her helplessness were unbearable.

Mrs. Monteeth said, ''You come and set down.''

''She don't look good,'' Gust said.

Moon spoke one rapid sentence.

"Yes," Sarah answered, mumbling. "Yes, I know I must be careful." She put her lips to the back of her hand. Stumbling, with Mrs. Monteeth helping her, she got back to the big room and she sat down by the dead fire.

Moon was behind her, jabbering. Sarah sat still. "Do nothing. Sit still. Go not into the dark night, young woman." Was that the sense of it? "Be wary of the old man." Sarah stretched her eyes, trying to get hold of the world.

The sight of Grandfather's study door was a release. She began to think of the old man's health. "Oh, what is she saying to Grandfather? He mustn't hear all this. He has to be protected. Oh someone . . . get the doctor here."

Gust looked at his wife and she said, greatly daring, "I think so. Yes, I think so. Gust, do you think so?"

Gust said, "What's the doctor's name? How'll I get ahold of him?"

"Price." Mrs. Monteeth bustled. "Probably in the book. Maybe a night number."

Sarah, snatching in all her whirling thoughts, at one, knew that authority and sanity were needed in this house. The doctor was not enough. She did not know where David was. But he was not enough either. He would be nearly as helpless as she was. He had chosen to lie to Malvina. (There was a reason, of course. She believed that. Must believe it.) But there needed to be judgment. Someone whose duty it was to distinguish the truth from the lies.

Sarah said in a low voice, "Moon, go call the man at the gate. Get him in here."

The Chinaman spoke. "They are trying to kill you," she understood him to say.

223

"Yes, I know they are," she said, repeating the sense she got of his plural subject without thought.

The Chinaman touched her shoulder in compassion. Then he ducked away.

In the study now a lamp burned. Grandfather stood in the middle of the room and his hands were soiled. Dirt crusted his fingers and the small vial in his right hand.

"You . . . stupid!" he raged. His voice was low and venomous.

"Suicide," said Malvina, eyes glistening. "David betrayed her. The servants told her so. Now. *Now*, when the motive is perfect!"

"You fool!" said Fox. "Go down the beach path."

"What?"

"At the first turnback you will find wire. Destroy it. Throw it over. You fool! Had you let her go she'd have fallen!"

The lines of Malvina's face sagged. "You didn't tell me, Grandfather."

"Tell *you!*" he raged.

"I thought, at dinner time . . . when you failed . . ."

"Failed!" he snarled. "I do not fail! *You interfere!*"

She swallowed.

"Now, hurry. Undo my trap, you big fool Malvina. Before people come. David, to see where she's got to. Or the police. There can be no trap on that path now. That much you have the sense to see. Go. Take it away."

"Yes, Grandfather," she said blankly.

"I have the poison in my hand," Grandfather said. "You have made such a mess of everything, now I must use it. And I did not wish to poison Sarah. I don't like it, Malvina. I have an instinct against it. But get on. Go. Hurry."

"The first turn?" she said stupidly.

"The highest, naturally," he snapped. "And if you fail in this, Malvina, I will kill you. I would be well rid of you."

"Sorry." She looked like a shell. The animus was out of the body.

"You may well be sorry," he said viciously. "Simplicity. Simplicity. But not for you. You have ruined my plans, every one. You and your lies and your stupidity. You are not clever, Malvina, and never will be. Get down that path."

Malvina said drearily, "How I used to try to think that you must love greatly to kill someone and then die. It is not so. You are sick and disgusted. That's all. And so was my father."

"Your father was a fool. Do as I say."

"No. He wasn't clever, was he?" Her eyes were strange. "And you didn't care for him."

"*Do as I say,*" he snapped for the last time.

She said nothing. She went out upon the sea walk.


At the base of the cliff Consuelo stood within the boulder's shelter. Her bare feet were icy from the water. She had got around the rock all right, with the tide out. Yes, this was the tiny private beach. And no one here.

Consuelo was frightened for Sarah Shepherd. She looked above her and saw where the path snaked upward. She was stout and sixty-two years old and it was a terrible climb. Still, it did not look steep, only narrow. Always at the sea side there would be the dizzying emptiness. Still, one could climb close to the inner side and if one did not look . . . after all, it was dark or at least darkish. . . . Her old heart gave a lurch of fear.

But Davey said the girl was to come this way and she hadn't. Consuelo had promised. She had never been one to break her promises.

Up there was the house and those wicked people. Something had to be done, no doubt of that. Consuelo shivered. She buttoned her coat carefully all the way down so that it could not flop about her body. She set her cold bare aching old foot on the path.

Well, who knows? thought she. I may, this night and in this place, leave the world and know it not again. Consuelo grinned in the dark. On the whole, she'd had a very good time. She'd enjoyed it. Now she tested the sensation of her heart beating, pulled air into her lungs.

Sixty-two, damned old fool, ought to be home in bed. Also her hair needed a little retouching at the part and for this she was regretful. Still, she was wearing her Paris petticoat. That's right, Consuelo. Weigh one thing against another. Do you or don't you mind risking your life, this evening?

She looked up. Well, no matter. She began to climb.

# Chapter 20

The doctor's wife was in another room watching television and the doctor was anxious to get to the program. His patience was superficial and would not last. David found himself stumbling over long, involved and unconvincing explanations. He cut them off. He smoothed down the lock at the crown of his head. "I see I'm getting no place and I don't know how to proceed, either. After all, what *could* a doctor notice that other people can't see?"

"A great many things," the doctor said a trifle huffily. The man had a small neat moustache on his taut intelligent face. His eyes were measuring rather than receptive.

"Dope addict?" said David, lifting an eyebrow.

"That I could notice. Mr. Fox is not a dope addict. I think it is within the bounds of professional conduct to tell you so." The doctor produced a mechanical smile. "Now, if you'll excuse me . . ."

"What could it be?" David thrust both hands into his pockets and took a turn on the doctor's hall runner. "It may only be, of course, that he isn't as sick as everyone had been told he is." To this the doctor said nothing. "You can't help me?"

"I don't see how, Mr. Wakeley. Since I don't know what you are asking, and neither do you."

"I'm asking for a sign, for evidence of some kind."

"Evidence of what?" The doctor was really annoyed. "Evidence of the state of his health, yes," he snapped.

"You examined him thoroughly?" The doctor gave him an icy stare. "He wasn't tattooed?" said David wildly.

"If you are pulling my leg," the doctor said, "I don't appreciate it. You can't seriously mean that you suspect that old gentleman of murder."

"I do. Yes, I do seriously suspect him."

The doctor spread his hands. "That would not be one of the things a doctor could see. I am hardly a criminal psychologist."

"He's not *younger* than he says? Anything like that?"

The doctor closed his mouth.

"Even if you had seen something, you wouldn't tell me," said David. "All right. I'm sorry. I'd hoped for some kind of break, some clue. . . . Something about his past, perhaps?"

"Now what . . . ?"

"A mark?" said David desperately. "Anything? I believe him to be behind the poisoning of a doctor. Dr. Perrott. Don't you doctors stick together? You are willing to take over the patient, not caring what happened to your predecessor?"

"Why would he poison Dr. Perrot?" said Dr. Price skeptically.

"That is what I need to know," said David. "*Why*. That is what the police want, too. The motive. I think there was something Dr. Perrot could *tell*. Some secret. Perhaps something only a doctor could see."

"Nothing like that," the doctor said. "Not a thing. The only mark he has is something anyone could see. That woman, the housekeeper, his granddaughters, I suppose, any nurse he ever had. There is surely no . . ."

"What mark is this?" David said. "I have never seen a mark."

"Not visible when he is clothed. Scar caused by a fall on the rocks, they tell me. It couldn't be that, of course. No, there is nothing at all."

"But there *is* a scar?"

"That, yes." The doctor nibbled his lips.

"Where is this scar?"

"It can't possibly be a secret," the doctor said angrily. "It's ten inches long, across his chest."

David sat down.

The doctor forgot the TV show. He looked at David's face closely. Then he, too, sat down and waited quietly.

"Tweedledum," said David in a moment, "looks very much like Tweedledee. Isn't that so?"

The doctor had more sense than to answer.

"In fact, there's not a pennyworth of difference between them." David's fist struck his thigh. "Many people must have seen them on the stage. But theatrical make-up is very heavy on a pair of clowns. And I myself saw the photographs. Now wait . . . wait . . ."

The doctor waited.

"Sarah has seen them perform. Sarah was in England. Malvina met her as a child. As a child . . . *as a child!*" David jumped up. "Consuelo will *know!* Thanks, thanks, thanks."

"What did I do?" The doctor was softened and full of curiosity.

"You did it! I think so. It was an arrow. An arrow! *She* did it with her little bow and arrow! Or if she didn't, at least she *saw* it! Consuelo was *there*. Now wait a minute. Sarah was there, too. I remember Consuelo saying she might have met the daughter. And if the daughter was there, so was the little girl. The little girl was Sarah. As a child."

"What do you mean? What are you on to?"

"I mean . . . Oh no, it's impossible. But if it's so . . ." David bit the edge of his palm. "If it's so, then Fox is *not Fox*. If he is not Fox, he's got to be Lupino. Why did Lupino want to be Fox? The California land! That's why!"

The doctor said in all good humor, "Steady."

"Yes, I know, but to go on steadily," said David slowly, "then Malvina is really his granddaughter. Then Sarah is not. Then *Sarah should have all the money!*" David thumped his palm. "It may seem impossible but it's got to be so."

The doctor exhaled loudly.

"Let me try this on you." David turned and now he watched and measured the doctor's reaction. "There's Fox and Lupino, a comedy team, alike as two peas. Now Fox had made investments. Suppose Fox dies in the blitz? And Lupino sneaks out of England, saying he's Fox? And saying it was Lupino that died. Why? Because of the investments. He could do it. He'd know enough for all the necessary faking. He had help. He had his own granddaughter.

"Well, then, what do they do? Why, they hole up far, far away from England and yes . . . exactly! They invent a heart so conveniently wonky that nobody gets in to see the old man except when he

230

says so. And nobody gets in *at all* who might know Fox and Lupino too well. That's it! *Consuelo couldn't get in.* And that does it, Doctor."

"You're talking about an impersonation, a fraud to get hold of property?" Dr. Price was following intently.

"I am. I am indeed. And Sarah Shepherd is not only the legitimate heiress to the property but she . . . Oh Lord, it must be so! She is the one who could expose the fraud."

"What makes you imagine . . . ?"

"Listen. That scar. It didn't happen on any rocks. Listen, years ago a small child shot an arrow into *Lupino's* breast."

The doctor said, "I see what you're after."

"Funny, huh? Both men, scarred breasts. Do you believe that? No, no. It must have been Sarah. At least they are afraid she can somehow spoil it. Maybe she doesn't know that this old man has a scar. She can't know it. Well, there it is. She mustn't know, mustn't remember, mustn't tell. Scare her away. Or, now, she'd better die. May I use your phone?"

"What are you going to do?"

"Calling Maxwell. Sheriff's Deputy. I've got his motive for him."

"Just a minute, Wakeley. You don't know this Sarah is the child who shot the arrow."

"No, but I believe it," David said. "And we can ask her."

"Look here, you are making a guess. You better go easy."

But David was getting Maxwell's private number and then calling it. "Maxwell? Wakeley. I've got the motive. Got the whole thing. It's a gigantic fraud. Sarah Shepherd could expose it. So there's your motive."

"That so?" said Maxwell, unimpressed. "Motive for what? Perrott's death?"

"Now listen, I can expose the poisoner of Dr. Perrott and I can expose this fraud, and I am going to do it. As soon as I pick up a couple of witnesses. If you want to watch me do it, better go up there."

"Up to the Nest, eh?"

"Right."

"What's it about?"

"You wouldn't believe me on the phone."

"Come down to my office."

"Nope. I need the old man."

"Why?"

"For evidence," said David.

"Evidence? What are you driving at?"

"Headlines," yelled David. "Professor bares criminal plot. You better see the show."

He hung up and the doctor said, "Will he go up there?"

"Wouldn't you?" said David. "Now I've got to have Sarah, and Consuelo, too. See you later and thanks. Thanks a million."

"Wakeley, if you're wrong you are going to run into plenty of trouble."

But David flung out of the doctor's house to Consuelo's car and roared into motion.

The doctor worried his moustache. Then his phone rang. "Yes?" he said. "Who? Fox? . . . Why yes, I'll be right along. . . . Certainly," he said with a good deal of enthusiasm. But when he hung up his eyes were uneasy.

David raced down Consuelo's street. Consuelo's house was silent and empty. No one was there.

David looked at his watch. The time he had taken was long enough. His heart rode in his throat as he drove swiftly to the other side of the Cove and parked on the highway's shoulder. His shadow pulled up behind him. David paid no attention. Consuelo's car stood there. It was empty and silent. No one was in it. No one was even near it.

David started to run on the sand.

He heard screaming.

# Chapter 21

Sarah sat alone in the inglenook and did not move, because she did not know what to do or where to go. The Monteeths were whispering in the foyer. Malvina was no doubt whispering to Grandfather in the study. Where David was, she did not know. Perhaps he was whispering to somebody.

She was not afraid. The doctor would come, and the guard from the gate. Malvina had tried to kill her, but Sarah did not think she would be killed. Malvina had tried to torture her with lies, but Sarah resolved to *think*. To believe in reasons and to wait for reasons. But it was very lonely where she was.

When the study door opened she clasped her hands gratefully. It was Grandfather himself who came trotting across the floor and he was quite calm.

He had a glass in his hand, a small heavy glass, and he came briskly to her, all fuss and concern, but he did not seem oppressed or sad. "Now, dearie," said Grandfather, "now we must hearten you in all this trouble. Where is everyone? Ah . . ."

"Where is Malvina?"

"Oh, I have scolded Malvina."

Sarah's heart lifted. She smiled at the dear old man.

"Mrs. Monteeth," called Grandfather. "Dear ma'am, fetch this child some drinking water."

Mrs. Monteeth scurried. "Doctor's coming up, sir," Gust said gruffly.

Grandfather seemed to bristle. His head went back on the neck and stayed, rigid. But he said calmly, "Ah yes. Yes, that is wise. He must see to Sarah, of course. Your coat on, dearie? Why yes, you are cold. You are shivering. Come, you must have this brandy." He beamed and set the glass down at Sarah's elbow. He touched her cheek. His finger was damp and smelled of soap. "Gust . . ."

Grandfather trotted and he and Gust were whispering in the foyer.

Sarah picked up the little glass. Now she felt again as if she were sinking under a weight. She was borne down to despair. How futile for Sarah's heart to lift, poor thing. While people whispered and eyes were solicitous upon her and everyone, even Grandfather, was sorry for her. When, although to her best understanding she had never in all her life meant to hurt anyone nor had she tried to hurt herself, yet trouble and tragedy followed her everywhere. Even David nagged them to get her to a psychiatrist. Her best understanding, then, couldn't be much good. *Stop it, Sarah. You know Malvina is a liar. Remember what you know. Remember what you don't know. Reason.*

But the thought came woefully, What is the reason that they lie to me and about me? Why should that be?

She straightened her back. "Grandfather . . ."

"Yes. Yes, my poor Sarah." He came and put his hand on her hair.

"Malvina, David, one of them or both of them . . . People are lying."

"Drink the little brandy, dearie. It will do you good."

"You never lie to me, Grandfather, at least. Tell me what I must do."

"First you must feel better," said Grandfather softly. It seemed kind and wise and she lifted the little glass, but someone was screaming and she did not drink any of the brandy. The glass jerked in her hand and, lest it spill on the carpet and on her skirt, she put it down.

Grandfather was bristling. The long scream died. Out on the sea side? Alarmed for the old man, Sarah jumped up. "I will see. I will see. It may be nothing at all. Grandfather, don't think about it. Take the brandy." Mrs. Monteeth came tottering in and Sarah cried to her to stay with the old man and, released from the paralysis, ran toward the study through which she could get outside.

But Gust Monteeth pounded behind her. He took her shoulders, put her aside and brushed by. The study was empty. Gust rushed on through and out of the door to the cliffside. Sarah herself was as far as that door when a strange man took her shoulders and he, too, set her aside and went by, saying, "Stay where you are, Miss. Don't get in the way."

He was the guard from the gate whom Moon had summoned, for Moon was behind him. Moon, too, brushed by.

Sarah peered out the open door, her fingers tense on the wood of its frame. She could hear shouting, men's voices calling and answering. But she could not see over the edge anything but the ocean, spreading endlessly. She stepped over the sill.

Yet another pair of hands took Sarah's shoulders. It was the Deputy, Maxwell. Big and angry. "What's going on out here? Where's Wakeley?"

"I don't know."

"Go sit down some place before you fall down," he told her brusquely. "Better get back inside." He was away.

The cliff path, the whole cliffside must be alive with people. Authority had come. Whatever had happened would be dealt with. She heard Maxwell bellow. A voice answered. "Woman . . . fell . . ."

There was no woman but Malvina.

Nothing out here for Sarah to do. She remembered how when Edgar and the car had fallen, many people had gone to do what they could. But Sarah had not gone. "Why, I must stay with Grandfather," she thought, rallying. "At least I can do that as I did before." So she turned into the house knowing only that Malvina had fallen, and she went back into the big room.

He sat in the inglenook and she thought his small figure looked lonely. She ran to him and knelt to see his brooding face. "Grandfather, are you all right? Oh how could they leave you? Where is everyone?"

"What is it, Sarah? Is it Malvina? What has Malvina done?" He spoke rather angrily.

"Grandfather, I'm afraid Malvina has fallen."

"How far?" he asked.

But Mrs. Monteeth now came announcing the doctor.

"Oh Doctor," Sarah rose, "will you please see if my grandfather is all right. This is so bad. This is so terrible for him.''

The doctor looked at her intently. But Fox said, "Malvina has been hurt out on the cliff. They'll need you *there,* Doctor."

"What? Hurt do you say?"

"Someone was screaming," Sarah told him. "I think she fell."

The doctor gave her an odd look. "How do I get out there?"

Mrs. Monteeth said, "I'll show you, Doctor." They went rapidly toward the excitement.

Sarah sat down on Malvina's stool. The little glass of brandy, still full, rested on the low coffee table. The old man sat on his cushions. The little blonde girl hid her fright and her confusion as best she could. All the violence and exertion, and the life and endeavor, all the hope and struggle seemed to be far away. Only these two remained beside the dead fire, calm and ignorant. An ancient man removed from the action, insulated by the experiences of his years, by the frailty of his body from the trouble, whatever it was. And a girl who saw things happen all around her but was, herself, somehow left in stagnant places. Because she was haunted.

Sarah thought, I might as well be old. I might as well be locked up somewhere. My life might as well be over. She did not know that her death . . . in a glass of brandy . . . was not four inches from her hand.

But Sarah fought. Made her mind move the only way it could go. Think of Grandfather's comfort. He could not be taken to his bed. The bedroom windows looked directly on the cliff side where some dreadful thing had happened.

239

"Grandfather, lean back," said Sarah, "and sip the brandy. Please do. Perhaps this is nothing so bad."

He said, "I suppose Malvina has done some stupid thing. Am I alone now?" His chin sank on his breast.

"No, no. I am here. I won't leave you."

His brows moved, corrugating his forehead. "Dear Sarah," he said, "you don't look well. You are white. Your color is bad."

"I'm all right. What can I do, Grandfather, to make this easier for you?"

"Drink the brandy," he murmured.

"I will," she said, smiling and picking up the glass. "I will if we make it a loving cup. If *you* will take some. Please, Grandfather?"

He closed his eyes. His lids shut down swiftly. "Sarah," he burst, "how is it that you cannot tell me? Go and inquire. Go, look over the edge and tell me. I am calm. I wish to know. Here is my whole house rocking about me and I do not know anything. Malvina fell? Well then, is she hurt? Is she dead? Perhaps . . ." He began to struggle. "I shall go myself."

"No, no . . . I'll go. I'll find out," Sarah said. "Grandfather, don't move. Don't upset yourself."

She didn't look back. She didn't see the old man's face as he slipped off the cushions and rose and followed.


Out on the sea walk again, Sarah crept to the edge and crouched down with her hands on the ground. Her forearms pained her as she leaned upon them. Whatever dim shapes were on the rocks or the path or the house level, it was a group in the bright circle of flashlight beams that Sarah could see. They were clustered on the path only a short way down from the brink upon which she hung.

There was a woman lying there and a man held her in his arms. His head . . . it was David Wakeley's head. The voice murmuring endearments and tenderness was David's voice. By the pose of the head, the caress of the hands, no one watching could doubt that the woman in his arms was one he deeply adored.

Sarah's heart winced. She, Sarah, was alone. She did not even know who it was that he loved so much and held so tenderly. Sarah, kneeling on the brink, was aware of the dark water.

She saw the doctor gesticulating. Then she saw David's head lift suddenly. He looked up. She heard his shout. "Sarah?"

"David." Her voice was lost in the vast emptiness of air.

"Go in. Into the house. Wait for me."

It was a shout. A loud shout it had to be to carry over the sea's noisy tumbling. A shout holds no nuance, cannot be tender or kind or even sorry. All shouts in a noisy night sound brusque or angry.

David saw the outline of her head against heaven begin to draw back and be hidden by the sharp line of the upper edge and he looked down into the light. "Consuelo darlin', are you feeling better?"

For three awful minutes David had been running toward a hole in the world where some screaming had been, thinking that the thing fallen from so high and now broken and silent across a rock was Sarah Shepherd.

But it was Malvina Lupino.

Then his shadow, Maxwell's man, had come behind him and Gust had come skittering down, crying that another woman lay fainting on the path. And he had climbed, thinking it would be Sarah Shepherd's unconscious body.

But it was Consuelo's.

So he held Consuelo and watched and hoped for her recovery, and people had come. None Sarah.

What made him look up and see her small neat head, a silhouette balanced dangerously in the sky, he would never know. But he shouted. She heard. David was not afraid for Sarah any more. She had gone where it was safe. The police were here. Malvina dead. The old Fox surrounded by people. It was all over.

So he kept murmuring and kept watching the exhaustion that frightened him on the beloved face and for which he was blaming himself. . . .

Sarah, withdrawn from the edge but still kneeling, looked over her shoulder. A small figure flitted past on the walk in the poor light. It was Moon. He was exhorting someone to go into the house. Scolding and berating. Why, it was Grandfather! So desperate for news as to have come himself! But how impudent of Moon to speak to him so. Oh, the old man who had come all the way to the outer door of the study must not step nearer, where Sarah was, on the cliff edge! No, thought Sarah, it's too dangerous! Suppose in weakness he staggered? He might fall!

Sarah sprang up. She did not yet understand what had happened to Malvina. Or to this woman beloved of David. But she knew her own duty.

Someone must look after Grandfather. Moon had already persuaded him back into the house and as Sarah braced herself to step over the threshold she saw Mrs. Monteeth now teetering toward her on the walk.

"What happened, Mrs. Monteeth?" cried Sarah. "Please, do you know?"

"Miss Malvina. Miss Malvina is killed. She went over. Down on the rocks. Miss Malvina, too." In the light from the house the housekeeper's flabby face was full of suspicious horror. "Like she *said*. Something terrible. Something terrible is going to happen to all of us around you."

Mrs. Monteeth shrank from Sarah's hand and brushed by, making whimpering noises. Then Gust followed, elbowing Sarah rudely. "Now, listen," he grabbed his wife, "no hy-sterics." His eyes turned. "Somebody's got to get her off to our room. She can't take no more." Sarah saw in his eyes the same horror.

Sarah felt leprous. She put her arm over her face. She heard the sounds they made, whispering and weeping, and then there was silence and she knew she was alone.

Only one place where Sarah could go, be wanted, be useful. She must go to Grandfather. So Sarah steadied herself, thinking, I can do this one time more. Next time, it won't work. I won't be able to do it. She went into the big room, marching, one more time.

Moon was pushing Grandfather back upon his cushions. The Chinaman turned and chattered a long stream of words and Sarah understood none of them. "Leave him to me," she said firmly, pretending a great competence. "I'll take care of him. I'll give him the brandy."

Moon stood quite still. Then he grinned and nodded.

"The doctor. . . ." said Sarah faintly.

Moon's head bobbed. He said one quick harsh sentence and Sarah nodded, automatically. Moon went away, back into the study. He thought he had warned her. She thought he had gone to fetch the doctor. She hadn't understood a word he had said.

"The news is so dreadful," said Grandfather plaintively, "that I am not to be told?" His eyes peered through his fingers.

"It's dreadful." Sarah knelt down. "Malvina fell over. Malvina is dead. But I will never leave you," she cried, not knowing what else to say.

"Ah, Sarah," said the old man. "We two, eh? Are you all right, my dearie? You won't faint?"

"No. I am strong," she said and she smiled fondly.

Grandfather sighed.


They were bringing Consuelo up into the study, David and Maxwell and Dr. Price. The Chinaman slipped through the inner door and Maxwell said sharply, "Keep that door shut. And be quiet." They put her into Grandfather's chair and David knelt with his face near hers. "Are you better, darlin'?" he pleaded.

Dr. Price said, "She'll be all right now."

"Davey . . ." The old lady's lids moved.

"I want to hear this." Maxwell shoved the bright-eyed Chinaman aside.

"There was something stuck into the path," Consuelo told them. Maxwell swore under his breath. "You may well say so," nodded Consuelo, her voice getting louder. "And I said much the same or stronger. Of all the nasty . . ."

"Consuelo, did it scare you? Did you almost fall?"

"Well, no. Since I happened to be coming along up on all fours. You see, my head's not good for edges. Never was." David squeezed her hand. "No," she said, "the wire, whatever it was, didn't bother me. But I had to pull it out, Davey. Because I thought it was dangerous."

"Dangerous!" He kissed her hand. "How you ever got up there . . . !"

"I didn't make it."

"You darned near made it."

"Well, good for me." Consuelo's grin was nearly normal. "Anyhow, I got pretty dizzy after getting that wire out of the way. It fell with an awful nasty hurry, d'you see? I think I lay down against the ground. Maybe I fainted. I dunno. Well, pretty soon, here comes Malvina."

Maxwell swore again.

"She fell over me," said Consuelo. "There I was, lying in her way."

"How in hell . . . ?"

"Don't blame yourself," said David sharply.

"Oh, I don't," said Consuelo. "I do not. But it was darned strange." Consuelo struggled higher and David supported her. "Here she comes, dragging her feet. I tried to move. I croaked. My lord, Davey, I'm quite a hulk. Nobody can deny that. How could she miss noticing me? But she didn't seem to hear me or see me. She was deliberately dragging her feet, like a sleepwalker. So she went over, screaming." Consuelo shuddered.

"There was wire?" said Maxwell. "You mean

that? You tell me this path had a trap on it?"

"It sure did have a trap on it," Consuelo said, "and where is Sarah Shepherd?"

"That's the little blonde girl?" said the doctor. "She's in there. She's all right. Now, Mrs. McGhee . . ."

"Wait . . ."

"You are better," David accused her. "Consuelo, you foolish old darlin'."

"Yes, I'm better, Davey. And by gum," said Consuelo looking around her, "maybe I did it the hard way, but I got in."

Moon began to jabber and gesture toward the inner door where the doctor stood with his hand on the knob, hesitant, still listening. Moon gave up the effort as suddenly as he had begun it and ducked out the opposite door upon the sea walk. He pattered swiftly to his right, to get around through the garden. One of Maxwell's men stood in his way. "Now where do you think *you're* going?"

After a while Moon made a gesture toward the night sky, as one who submitted. He sat down on the flagstones and looked quietly off to sea.

In the study, David stood up. "I've got to go to Sarah. Maxwell, I hope you realize that they tried to murder her again."

Maxwell said, "They won't murder anybody. I'm going in there. I've got questions to ask."

So Maxwell opened the door. David could see through. He saw Sarah. She was sitting quietly on the stool where Malvina had sat so often. Her back was straight. Her head was high and steady. The big glasses gleamed owlishly. She was just there, solemn and sweet and composed. The door closed.

David bent. "Consuelo, that arrow? Who was the child? Was it *Sarah?*"

She stared at him.

"I thought you'd know. You told me about a child shooting an arrow. *This* man has a scar. I think this man is *Lupino.*"

Consuelo said, "Oh gosh, Davey . . . wait. Let me remember."

"It was a girl?" he prodded.

"Yes, of course. It was one of the granddaughters."

"Which one? Not Malvina?"

"Davey, I can find out. I can call somebody in London."

"Consuelo, did they look alike off stage? Fox and Lupino?"

"Yes, they did."

"Would *you know* Lupino from Fox?"

"I don't know." Her eyes were honest. "I might. But it's been years. I'm not sure."

Dr. Price said, "I'd advise her to rest."

Consuelo said, "Now, you keep quiet. Davey, tell me . . . can I do anything? Can I bluff it? Will that help you?"

# Chapter 22

Maxwell stalked across the living room. "Who fixed a trap on that path going down?" he demanded. "Who was trying to do murder out there?"

The little blonde girl said in a voice quite calm, "You mustn't speak so harshly, please. My grandfather isn't strong."

"Who was going to go down that path this evening?"

"I was," said Sarah.

"Somebody is trying to murder you?"

"Why, yes," she said. "Malvina is. Malvina Lupino."

"Now, is that likely," the Deputy scoffed, "when she is the one who fell and died?"

Sarah stood up without trembling, conquering her trembling once more. (Once more.) "This is not good for my grandfather. If you please . . ."

"Wait, Sarah," Grandfather said crisply. "Sit down, dearie, and let us examine these things. All of this must be settled. I am tired of crises. Now, how did you get here?" he asked the Deputy. "David Wakeley sent you, I suppose."

"That's right," said Maxwell.

Sarah began to tremble. She sat down.

"We have had enough trouble," said Grandfather. "And Malvina is dead? Speak bluntly."

"Yes. Dead. Fell all the way."

The old man put his hand over his eyes for a second's time. Sarah moistened her lips. Everything swirled in her mind. David had been the liar! David had called the police. David had not intended to run away with her. It was Malvina who had told the truth. He chose no bride in so silly a fashion. That too was true. This woman who lived down the shore, whose car he drove, the one he held in his arms right now out on the cliffside, *she* was his beloved. Well, if it was so . . . Sarah clenched her jaw to hold herself quiet . . . then it was so, and no shuddering could change it. But was there no one anywhere who always told her the truth but this old man on the cushions?

"What's going on up here, Mr. Fox?" said Maxwell. "Can *you* tell me?"

Grandfather said, "I'll try." He sighed. He looked slyly at Sarah's face. "Sarah, you must sit quietly. You must do nothing. Do not faint. Take the brandy. Now, sir."

Grandfather shifted. He kept his hand against his face as if he shielded his cheek from the fire, although there was no fire burning any more. Sarah sat on the stool and looked helplessly up into his face. "There has been too much trouble," Grandfather said. "This child had a bad experience. Her bridegroom fell dead—of a heart thing, they say—as they left the altar. She cannot be rid of it. She cannot shake off that ghost. She has come to believe that wherever she goes, goes tragedy."

"I've heard this before. First from Wakeley. Then from Miss Lupino." The Deputy was impatient.

Sarah saw that her fate was not in her own hands, not in her will. She understood nothing.

"Well, then," said Grandfather, "now we've done all we can. I asked Wakeley to come here because Sarah was drawn to him and I felt it would heal her." Sarah's lips fell open. "But the compulsion to punish *herself*, you see . . ." Sarah caught breath. "She set their working place on fire. Perhaps you know that," said Grandfather.

"That isn't true," said Sarah.

Grandfather didn't seem to hear. Perhaps she hadn't spoken. "Then poor Dr. Perrott, in love with Malvina, chose to drive himself over the road's edge and Sarah, of course, welcomed it. It seemed proof to her," said Grandfather, "that all she wished to believe was so."

"No," said Sarah. "No, I never wished . . ."

"Ah, dearie, so long we've watched it," said Grandfather sadly, "and *you* would not know."

She thought she was going to fall. She reached for the brandy.

"But Edgar was saved." Grandfather watched her sideways. "That was not in her pattern. Well, she had the poison . . ."

"I . . . did not have the poison," said Sarah.

"Wakeley realized how serious her state was," Grandfather went on speaking, "and urged psychiatric care. Oh, we were coming to it. And perhaps she knew this also." Grandfather sighed. "Sarah put the wire in the path, of course."

"But I . . . did not," said Sarah. "Why? Why?"

"In your mind, my poor Sarah," said Grandfather, "there *is* no reliable reason." He leaned forward, eyes keen. "I saw you from my room. On the sea walk, this afternoon, with the wire in your hands."

"Now you are lying, too," said Sarah faintly.

Grandfather did not move his eyes. "Ah, she says everyone is lying," he said softly, "all a part of this . . . Look out! Give her the brandy!"

The Deputy bent and his arm went around her. He took the little glass out of her numb fingers and Sarah felt it against her lips. "Come now," he rumbled. "Don't worry. Nobody's going to hurt you."

"Everyone says . . ." her mouth refused the glass to be able to speak, "things that are not true."

"Now, that's not the way to look at it, miss." The Deputy spoke one word, aside. "Paranoia?"

"Poor child," said Grandfather. "Poor, poor child . . ." and she saw his eyes.

Sarah straightened her back. Her hand struck the glass and it moved in the Deputy's hand as if on a hinge, away. She bent, feeling the Deputy's arm strongly holding her (and fighting to believe she was sane). Sarah peered upward. There was something she had seen before. Something she knew and had not seen in a long time. "Your eyes, Grandfather," she stammered.

His eyes were perfectly cruel.

Sarah swayed and the Deputy held her and the glass came up. "I don't want it," Sarah said. "I've got to think . . . because . . . everyone . . . really is . . . telling lies. . . ."

The liquid would have slopped into her mouth but she heard David saying in a firm commanding voice, "Open the old man's shirt."

So the Deputy turned. Grandfather leaned forward, one hand out. The Deputy's fingers

252

loosened and the old man took the glass. His head turned, eyes slid; the face was furious and evil.

Sarah knew that David was approaching. She saw that he had his arm around a stout blonde woman who walked . . . why, she was old! . . . who tottered, with her eyes fixed on Grandfather, slowly toward them.

Maxwell swore and his arm fell from Sarah's back.

Sarah turned her head again.

*"Grandfather,"* she cried, and fell to her knees in perfect panic. "Grandfather, what is the matter? *Why is your mouth the way it is?"*

The lips writhed and through the bad teeth, bitterly, viciously, the old man said, *"The better to eat you,* my dearie? Eh? Sarah?" And the little glass fell from his hand to the carpet.

"Get out of the way," the doctor said.

Maxwell lifted Sarah bodily.

Arms took her.

The doctor, working, giving orders, opened the old man's clothing.

"Look, Sarah," said David in her ear. "It was *all* a lie. Do you know that scar?"

"I remember it," Sarah said.

"Don't watch, then. The brandy was poisoned. He is dying." David's fingers pressed her face. His voice was tender and she was in his arms.


Consuelo McGhee's beach house was furnished in slap-dash elegance. Sarah rested there on a wildly flowered couch and watched Consuelo encourage the fire.

"I think I remember you," puzzled Sarah, "but why do I think of red hair?"

"No doubt because I had it," said Consuelo, "the week end of the arrow. Must have been your father I gave what-for?"

Sarah nodded.

"Your mama had the grand good sense to run away with him and get out of that. Might as well know that I don't think your own grandfather was a lot better than this one. They were very much alike, more ways than their looks, that pair. Don't blame yourself for being fooled. Lupino fooled everyone. Would have fooled me, too, as far as that goes. *I* wouldn't have sworn which one he was. So *old.*" Poking the fire, Consuelo shivered.

"I was in a state when I came here," said Sarah flushing, "and he was kind."

"Honey," Consuelo said.

"Yes, Mrs. McGhee?"

"He had to be kind. But it was just a legend. He was no ancient lovable clown. He was arrogant and wicked. You've been fighting alone too long and you didn't know what it was you were fighting, and it's not so good to be alone." Consuelo sat down and twisted her beads and something about her was wise and comical. "Now don't you mourn them, Sarah, those three. They couldn't stomach *themselves,* if you ask me. All three of them did themselves in, if you'll notice. Edgar must have known there was poison in the glass and knew who put it there. That's why he took it. And Malvina might as well have jumped. I told you."

"Yes."

"And the old man knew the brandy was poisoned. He planned it for *you.*"

"Yes, I know."

"Let's us be glad it's over," Consuelo grinned,

"and wait for Davey."

So David found them. "Tidied up?" asked Consuelo brightly.

"Fairly so." David sat down. He was tired. The Sheriff's Deputy had been a blaze of angry energy, beating about him for order and information, mad as a bee because he had almost poisoned Sarah Shepherd with his own hand. "How are you, Sarah?"

"Sarah's fine. We hashed it all out. It's all straight now." Consuelo's chins joggled.

Sarah said soberly, "It's hard to believe that they are all gone. The Nest is empty."

"Nest of snakes," snorted Consuelo.

"What a blood thirsty old critter this is," said David adoringly.

"I can't get over it," said Sarah, suddenly sparkling. "She climbed up that scary path for my sake and she doesn't even know me."

"Go ahead, make me a hero," beamed Consuelo. "I did it for Davey, you know."

"He doesn't know me, either," Sarah said.

"Well . . ." David smiled. "By the way, Sarah. Here is your Will. Shall we burn it?"

Sarah said, "That was silly. It's like waking up." She sat high and saw the paper flare. "It seems almost f-funny now. How you and I kept asking each other to get married. Whatever were we thinking of?"

David batted his lock desperately. Consuelo yawned. "What's that? Eleven-thirty! Past my bedtime. Good night, children."

Sarah watched her go. She turned to look at David and he was trying to bite a smile in two. "She's lying!" said Sarah.

"Yep."

"I bet it's not her bedtime. Oh, David, I could just adore her, too." Sarah's eyes filled with tears. "I don't know what to say to you. I hardly know where I am."

He picked up her hand, fearful for her still, wanting for her peace and balance. "You'll see," he murmured. "Work it out slowly. But there's nothing wrong. You *don't* bring bad luck. *Couldn't*. Will you hang on to that to start with?"

"I know I am lucky," she said solemnly.

He thought of the pressures she'd had upon her, the evil that had been all around her, and how this small body encased a spirit that had not broken. His eyes stung. "Meantime," he said cheerfully, holding back, "you know, I need a secretary."

Sarah's beautiful mouth twitched. "You *are* stubborn," it said.

He could see past the tears to the laughter and deeper. He looked at the mouth and held back no longer.